Inlands

Published by Nordisk Books, 2020
www.nordiskbooks.com

Elin Willows, 2018. First published by Natur & Kultur.
Published by arrangement with Partners in Stories
Stockholm, Sweden.

This English translation copyright
© Duncan J. Lewis, 2019.

Cover design © Nordisk Books
Cover art by Lise Blomberg

Printed and bound in Great Britain by Clays Ltd,
Elcograf S.p.A.

A CIP catalogue record for this book is
available from the British Library

ISBN 9780995485266

Elin Willows
Inlands

Translated by Duncan J. Lewis

nordisk books

Also by Nordisk Books

For my grandfather

Part one

1

In a place where people look at you. A place where it's apparent that I'm new. I have to explain in the grocery store – yes, I live here, I've moved here.

The occasional welcoming reply in return, but I don't feel accepted here. I understand that it will take more than that.

And next time I'm standing at the till comes the follow-up question: Why?

It's summer and most of the tourists are from Norway. They arrive throughout the day and stop outside the shop with their enormous cars.

Family size packs of bacon, mild cheese and Coke. And afterwards, at the till: How much is the Petterøe's?

It's half the price of tobacco in Norway. They're predictable, the Norwegians. They buy the same stuff every time and we laugh about it in the stockroom. Not because it's so hilarious, but there isn't that much else to laugh at. I don't know my colleagues. I know what they are called and where some of them live, but I know nothing about them. But I learn. Laila, who holds short speeches during the *fika* and lunch breaks, about how it was better in the old days and how we should all get that immigrants aren't doing our country any good. I think about how the only foreigners here are the Norwegians and wonder why no one argues with her. The others look away. Fredrik eats his snack consisting of canned tuna. Sometimes he puts the tuna on a cracker, other times he just eats it straight from the can with a fork. He doesn't sit with the rest of us at the table; he leans nonchalantly against the counter. He's usually the only guy.

I got the job here quickly. I had good references and Ann-Christine was retiring. After working here for a few months, I've become used to the routine. Deliveries are on Mondays and Thursdays and sometimes during the week we collect orders. They come in from older customers out in the neighbouring villages, those who aren't able to do the shopping themselves. Their detailed lists often include things like weekly magazines or a bag of boiled sweets, which I always pack last. Then I think about how Iris or Karl or Gertrud will enjoy them. This might be the highlight of their week.

One day, just as I've taken down a bar of chocolate and a magazine for someone called Siv, I decide that my week also needs a highlight. It's Saturday and the shop closes early, but the kiosk is open and I buy an interiors magazine and spend half an hour choosing pick 'n' mix.

The kiosk is known as 'Olle's' but it does have a proper name, which I can never remember. The other shoppers always pass a friendly greeting to the guy who may be called Olof, but even after six months of Saturdays I don't feel like one of them.

In both places, there's equal surprise. Not over the fact that I want to live with him, but that I'm the one moving to him. Everyone wonders why we don't do it the other way round. Why he doesn't move to me. The people I'm moving away from don't know where I'm going. No one has been here. Where I'm moving to, they're also surprised. Why am I leaving that which I'm leaving, for this? And, before it's over, the answer to the first question is him. And the answer to the second question is that we haven't even considered doing it the other way round. That somehow this made sense for us. Us. Which no longer exists. And so the astonishment only increases when I stay, when I decide to not move back. But there isn't a way back. I've made my decision and now I'll live with it until the next decision. And I'm not ready for anything like that right now.

That which was once our decision, now feels like a different decision, now that it's I alone who stand behind it. All that surprise is infectious. But at the same time, I become more sure of my choice. Or more sure that I'll stick with it.

2

One day when I finish early, Lena, who normally works on the meat counter, says that she's going to the flea market. She's worked the early shift and when she notices that I'm on my way out the door she asks if I want to come too.

We drive to the small industrial park, through gritted snow that's slowly melting away. It's the end of April and hard to believe that it will ever be summer in this place. I had been here previously, with him, before I moved up, but I don't remember it being so big. There are hundreds of pieces of furniture in the old warehouse. After a couple of laps, I decide to go for a small desk and a nightstand. I also find a rug for my large room and up against a wall there are VHS tapes loaded with home-recorded, British crime series. I choose seven tapes.

It's only when I get to the till that I realise I haven't seen prices on any of the items and it's clear that there aren't any when the man behind the counter asks what I'd like to pay. I'm confused by the question and finally name a price that the man at the till halves and rounds down.

Lena says that she'll happily drive me home as it's not really a detour – And you like crime shows I can see?

She's obviously referring to the VHS tapes and continues: Have you seen the Norwegian series, 'Murder Mysteries'?

I say that I must have missed it, and she explains that it's really good and that she actually has all the episodes taped, because it's on exactly when her son has football training that she has to drive him to. She says she'll bring the tape into work tomorrow if I'm interested.

The winter is so cold here, but somehow still warm. The cold gives a kind of security and there's no wind this far inland. The thermometer shows minus 28 and I have to buy new gloves. He drives me over to the neighbouring town. There are multiple shops to choose from and it can just about be considered a town. Now that we are no longer a couple, we talk differently to one another. Occasionally I almost forget to not use that voice which was only for him, but at the same time it feels good to avoid it. We can still talk to each other now, but not about the same things.

Even if my salary is low, I'm suddenly flush with money. I work five days a week, sometimes six and as I don't have a car, I rarely leave the village, where there are no shops in which to spend money. Maybe I should get my own flat. Mona, from whom I'm renting a room, has said I can stay as long as I like and that she hasn't planned on increasing the rent. It's too low and I'm not sure if she is aware of it.

And I'm happy there but I sometimes wonder how long she will be able to put up with that large house.

Everyone knows so much about cars here. When I have my lunchbreak at the same time as Stina and Fredrik, they only talk about alloys.

3

I read in the local paper about a snow scooter accident in the neighbouring town. About how someone never came home from a trip out and how someone else worried for hours before they found out about the accident. Those hours of distress are described in so much detail. It's almost as if I feel the panic myself while I read the article. It's a familiar but unusual feeling, it's been a while since I've felt it.

On the ice, I've often known the feeling, but it's a long time ago, I was last out on the ice when I was with him. Before I moved here. I could never imagine driving on the frozen lakes, barely walk out there. But neither do I have my license. And I rarely get in a car with anyone else now. I stay in the village. There's no anxiety here. No one I need to be anxious about. I've got myself. I avoid a lot of emotions by being here.

It's ten o'clock and my coffee break is over. Fredrik chucks two banana skins in the bin and I fold up the paper.

Nature surrounds this place, but I still don't make it out there. Not without a car. On my walks, I just wander around the village; I listen to music and lose track of time, especially now in the summer when the sun is constantly present. I walk along the streets and footpaths and along the roadside and I meet nobody and no flora.

Every now and then he calls and asks if I fancy going out. Then I say yes. We take the car and watch the country road verges flash by the windows, but the landscape barely changes. He usually chooses a layby next to the road, where he leaves the car, and we go for a walk.

This is where nature lives. This is where you find the tall trees, unfamiliar with cities and electric lights. This is where there are paths, created from years of arbitrary wandering, which criss-cross as they bed in. This is where there is a kind of freedom, which I haven't yet understood or made use of. A kind of freedom which is much clearer from a distance.

4

No one moves here. This becomes clear long before I pack up the car with all my things, to move here. It leads to countless explanations as to why I'm leaving the city to move more than a thousand kilometres away. Love, that's the simplest explanation. But it still seems odd that I'm moving. That's what everyone thinks.

After it's over, the best explanation is gone. It's in the air already while we're stuffing my things in the car. It's like playing Tetris, trying to get everything in the car, even with the estate we've borrowed. It's not that we're arguing, but the ambience between us has changed. Living together in the same town, which we've worked for, eventually turns out to be the thing that bursts the bubble. We make the journey up in one stretch. We'd planned to stay over with friends on the way, but I understand why he suddenly says: We might as well just drive the whole way now.

It's not a thousand unbearable kilometres. We know each other too well for it to be insufferable, but it's unnecessary.

I don't want to be the one who makes the first move, so I wait for him. It lasts about a week and my two rooms are inhabitable by the time he wants to speak. We don't need to say a lot to one another. The unsaid is said and we both realise that this doesn't change too much. And I end up staying; I've made my choice.

From time to time, I wonder what my teenage self would have thought of my moving here. Not because it's a long time since I was a teenager, but because it isn't. Some things change so quickly. Perspective can change.

I see the Northern Lights for the first time one evening when I've just started to get used to the loneliness. He calls me: You need to go outside now.

It's freezing cold, as I learn it is on these nights, and I have way too few clothes on. But I stay outside. Against my better judgment, I'm enchanted and end up walking down to the lake for a clearer view. The green lights have the upper hand tonight. They cover the whole sky. I think about how this is something that I'll want to remember and regret not having a camera with me, but immediately realise that it would never be the same in a photo.

The cold bites, so that the two pairs of gloves don't quite cut it and I wish I was wearing thermals. The evening air is a tight film over my face. Suddenly, he's standing next to me with a certain degree of anticipation, a certain degree of persuasion: 'You must love this?'

And I do.

I go home with him and we drink tea and

nothing more. Nothing more can happen between us ever again. We both know this, it's not in the air, not in our bodies.

On the way home, I feel a kind of gratitude. The Northern Lights ended some time ago and have left behind a huge star-speckled sky. If I was freezing before, the cold is painful now, and I hurry along the path through the village.

When winter comes, I've been living in the room I'm renting for a year. There are actually two rooms, but one of them is more like a hallway, and just contains my desk, where I also eat breakfast. I always have dinner in the bed which also functions as a sofa in the larger of the two rooms. I watch TV.

5

You need to find another way to make yourself tired in the summer. Something other than nightfall. Because it doesn't exist. We're south of the arctic circle, but the sun doesn't make it below the horizon before it's up again. The light does not sleep.

It takes a while to get used to the eternal daylight. To get used to the peculiarly transparent light at night time.

Blinds don't help. Eyes still too clear, alight.

I take the first paid leave of my life. Normally you'd have to wait until the second year of employment, but Sonia lets me take it anyway and suddenly I have two weeks without constraints. Two weeks with no outline.

The only thing I know is that I don't want to leave here during my holiday. I don't want to go home to my family yet and I can't get away from here without a car. I stay here and let the days pass. Days and nights. They melt together, with the constant light filtering through the rolled-down blinds.

At the start there were a lot of looks. Long held looks which stick to my skin afterwards. Stay in my head. Before too, when I was with him here, I got those looks, but he was like a shield. The looks bounced off him and they weren't as drawn out. I gained acceptance through him, because I was here with him. It went unquestioned, by his side I was welcomed. And he didn't get the looks because they could speak to him, ask him questions. I get questions too, but more often I get those looks. And without him I don't know who they are coming from.

I don't tell anyone that my reason for moving here has gone, not directly at least. Especially not my family. I can't be bothered trying to convince them or having to answer questions about when I'm coming home. This is my home now. I decided that a week after it was over. I'm here now.

I only tell them what's happened after I get the job. I tell them in a way that it's not quite clear when it happened. No one thinks to ask either and instead they tell me that I'm brave to stay here.

6

Calm on the lake. The great wide deep lake which gives the village a coastline that it doesn't really have. It's the evening and I go for a walk as usual, this time along the lake shore and he's with me. He has called earlier today and asked how I was doing and what I've been up to over the summer. I tell him I've been working and don't mention the holiday.

We haven't seen one another for a few weeks and he's tanned and wearing sunglasses, even though it's unnecessary in the evenings when the sun is lower. I realise that he wants to say something, tell me something. He passes his hand through his hair, builds up to it: Listen – I'm going to be moving.

He's got into a school I didn't even know he had applied at and he's moving to the coast, he tells me. The real coast, with a proper coastline. He hesitates, as if waiting for an approval from me, but I just say congratulations and that's great and I think I also mean it.

We walk for a while without saying anything and finally we've walked for hours and the sun creeps down but we both know that it'll soon turn and we turn and walk back to my place. He hugs me at the door and says bye.

And I know that it really is bye now.

I don't think any more about it that night and when I wake up the next day, I 've forgotten about it at first. It's only when I'm buttering my toast that I come to remember that he's leaving.

7

If you're going out, you go to the Hotel. And people do go out, but I don't. It's Saturday and I've been to the kiosk to buy a magazine and pick 'n' mix. I've got one of the VHS crime mysteries on the TV. I'm wearing jogging bottoms and a freebie promotional t-shirt. I'm just stuffing a foam strawberry into my mouth when the first murder takes place and there's a knock at the door. I pause the tape and assume it's either him or a wayward drunk. But it's Stina from work. Behind her in the autumn gloaming there's a car idling, its lights shining through the damp air: Hey, we're on our way to the Hotel and thought you might want to come along.

She was also working today, just like me and we didn't chat more than usual, but maybe she hinted at the fact that she was going out this evening and maybe I hinted at the fact that I might like to tag along. I notice her looking at my clothes, notice the artificial straw-berry taste in my mouth: I'll just get changed.

The guy driving the car is hopefully sober and introduces himself as Kalle. I recognise him of course, even if we've never spoken. You know people, here. I've met Stina's friend Jenny before, at the shop, and she sits next to me in the back in a short, black dress. On the floor of the car are beer cans and other rubbish, as well as Jenny's pin-sharp heels. The music is loud enough that we avoid having to talk. I close my eyes in the darkness.

You don't walk to the Hotel. You don't really walk anywhere here, but especially not to the hotel because it's at the top of the hill. The view is described with words like breathtaking and it's not far from the truth if you're into nature. Of course you can see the whole village from here, but you can also see how small it is. From here you understand that the area is dominated by nature. The lake, the mountain, the wide vistas, the forest.

Kalle parks and we go in. We leave our jackets in the car but cold skin soon warms up, becomes almost clammy, it's a full house tonight. It's packed every Saturday and I recognise almost everyone here. They're either customers or they work at the petrol station or friends of these people that I don't know personally.

Two texts when the news has gotten out. From home. One comforting and the other more questioning; you'll be coming home now? But I'm not. That's the one thing I've made my mind up about. I answer both briefly. A thanks and an explanation that I have a job here now.

When I worked out the explanation, it was clear in my mind and when someone calls to ask the same question afterwards, it sounds true when I give the same answer.

Before I moved here, my winters were dreich and lacking snow and I know it'll be different here. That the temperature is always below zero and it snows relentlessly. There is no spring here but instead there is a proper winter. Snow, cold, darkness. At the beginning, fifteen below feels cold, but everything is relative and after a while minus 20 becomes the new norm. And not even that cold.

8

The first snow arrives in October and doesn't leave before April; sometimes there's a flurry during the end of term presentations. That's why my first autumn is short, the snow falls in October. I struggle with it and think about the rainy evenings that don't exist here. The snow packs the village in and eventually those thoughts of rain are excluded. They don't fit in here.

Occasionally, I go back to my old home. Sometimes I fly from the neighbouring town, but usually I take the bus to the coast and then the train. It takes so long, and I know that's why I prefer the train.

It's always a night train and it's difficult to sleep the whole night. In our compartment there are six bunks and tonight, on the way home to that which is now home, I'm lying on the middle bunk and listening to music. I'm wearing thermal underwear and socks, a vest and a cardigan but I can still feel the cold creeping in under the felt with which the railway company has lined the bed. I've given up trying to get to sleep tonight and the guy singing in my ears is singing about unrequited love.

The bag at my feet is bigger than when I travelled south and it already feels like it was ten years ago that I was in my old home. That world seems so disconnected from my life now. My two lives, completely separated, connected only by the fact that I live in both of them. I think about my old life in a large city as a vacuum that I can still go into, but when I'm there, my current life becomes strange and unreachable.

I dig out my great big scarf and wind it round my shoulders and neck and at some point in the night I'm dragged into sleep, with the music still playing in my ears. I dream about summer and when I awaken they're calling my station: The train will be stopping in five minutes.

My backpack is heavy, full of uneaten food and dirty laundry. But there are also unread books and types of tea that you can't get where I live now. A taste of the old life.

The coastal winter is completely different, even if the latitude is about the same. The cold here is raw and aggressive, with a biting wind. I walk the hundred metres to the bus station, still sleepy in spite of the fact that it's 20 below. The bland building welcomes me with its warmth; I sit down on a bench and close my eyes.

First I feel the smile, then I open my eyes. I almost feel the warmth of another person but mainly it's the smile. Fredrik is sitting next to me on the bench: Are you sleeping?

I say no but it can't be right, one of the two hours' waiting time has already gone. He was at a friend's house over the weekend and is taking the same bus as me, so I coil up my headphones and pack them away.

The bus journey feels both longer and shorter than usual. First of all, a rather tentative discussion about how we spent the part of the journey prior to taking the bus, but then suddenly the conversation opens out and I know his grandmother's name and how much he can bench press.

We don't sit next to each other, he sits in the row in front, turned back towards me. I don't have to decide how we should sit, as I get on first. Occasionally he turns towards the window and goes silent for a moment, but then I see in his reflection in the window that he's thought of something and he turns towards me again. He declines when I offer him sweets from the pick 'n' mix bag, which I know he will – he doesn't eat anything with sugar in it, he's on a strict diet and adheres to a strict training schedule.

After a few hours on the bus, the sun starts to go down and I begin to feel tired.

Fredrik wakes me when we're swinging into the town square. He says my name softly and I hear him before I open my eyes. I sling my bag over one shoulder and get off the bus, Fredrik following: Do you want a lift?

My bike is parked nearby and I try to unlock it after I've said no, but it's too cold and Fredrik laughs a little at me, but in a kind way: You know that no one locks their bikes here, right?

9

Would you like a good winter coat? Lena suddenly asked me one lunchtime.

I look up from a gossip magazine I was buried in to see if it really is me she is talking to. She tells me that her sister had given her a coat that turned out to be too small and she had thought of me. It's the middle of summer and I don't think to ask about it and just say yes.

The next day, she has the coat with her in a bag. It's not really something I would have chosen myself, but then I'm not sure what I would have chosen. I haven't bought myself clothes since I moved here.

It fits perfectly and it's warm and I immediately realise that I will stay here this winter too. It's not something I'd previously thought about. I've neither thought about moving or staying, but when I thank Lena for the coat, I know that I'll be staying another winter.

It could have been a much bigger deal, the fact that we broke up. But given that the plan was always that I'd live on my own here, there were no logistics to worry about. No keys to hand back, no clothes or other stuff to collect, not even a toothbrush. That's why he disappears so quietly, he's simply gone, physically, but to start with he's still present. Of course, this is because of the place. The place which only existed for me because of him. Which should have been a meaningless spot on the map, or an unknown name, if we had not met. He is the place and the place is him. That's why in the beginning I think to myself that I need to create my own idea of the place that I have moved to, where I've ended up. But it is difficult and not because of my half-arsed efforts, rather the size of the community. Whatever I do, my image of this place will not change much when there are so few alternatives. No other roads to take than those we took, no places to visit other than those I visited with him. And he is still here. Is still a part of this place, even if we don't see one another much.

10

I understand that what would be spring in another landscape, here is a kind of transitional period. It coincides with my self-chosen loneliness crossing over into unwanted isolation.

To start with, everyone else at the driving school is younger than me, but after a while some older people join too. Although I understand swiftly that the other mature students are not from round here. They've come to get their license quickly, maybe in a fortnight, as there is not much else to do so they can focus single-mindedly on the license. The younger ones, those who live here, almost always pass first time.

I pass first time too, but not for the same reason, I guess. It's not at all easy for me. Not to start with. Sitting behind the wheel of a car is a foreign environment. I'd never gotten in on this side of the car, never got to drive a bit for fun on a deserted road, never even seen a deserted road before I came here. I'm more like the ones here on the intensive course. If I hadn't moved here, I might never have taken a driving test at all. Now I'm reading the theory book when I go to bed.

The conversation on our *fika* breaks is about cars, the amount of snow, local gossip, news about the neighbouring town, updates from the coast, complaints about customers, complaints about pretty much everyone. Laila is the boss of whining. She puts so much energy into complaining about people that it fascinates me.

She is looking for support and tries to obtain it by eye contact. Not from Fredrik and I. Fredrik's position by the counter gives him a certain distance. My distance is not physical.

11

I go with Stina and Jenny to the Hotel every week now. It's not something we decide, but it just ends up happening and they come to pick me up every Saturday. I end up recognising the sound of the engine of Kalle's car; he always drives.

I know that the Hotel is the sort of place I would never have gone to if it wasn't right there.

I'm past all the questions and when someone asks me something now, I'm out of practice with coming up with an answer. Everyone knows where I come from and there's nothing else to tell. Nothing I want to tell. I have nothing to hide but nothing to brag about.

Fredrik eats half a grilled chicken for lunch and I have an instant soup. He turns to me from his place at the counter: Are you just having a break here then, or have you moved here full time now?

I've been living here for more than a year when he asks this and I understand that it's the least of things. That I should have managed to make my mind up properly after so long. That I'm not just trying it out, testing myself, but someone who actually wants to live here. Of course he knows my original reason for moving here and he knows that reason has gone, but he does not know, no one knows, why I stayed. I don't answer the question directly, but only say what we both already know, that I've lived here for more than a year now. I look out over the carpark outside the window, the snow piling up round Fredrik's expensive car. I'm not ready for the question, I'm not ready to come up with an answer.

12

The least surprising thing here is the cold. You can guess that from looking at the map. The village's location in terms of latitude, in relation to the arctic circle. And that's one of the first things he says to me when we have become we and when we talk about my visiting him: You know that the winters are proper cold here?

And I know it subconsciously, but the cold here is unimaginable for someone who comes from a thousand kilometres away. Someone like me. Who has never experienced a winter which doesn't hold back, a cold which will not wait and a darkness which never lets go. But in the main, it's a matter of getting used to it. Not everything, but most things, you can get used to after a while. The darkness becomes normal, the cold is not unusual and his accent, which sounded so strange at first, over the phone, becomes recognisable and even comforting.

I come across an apartment for rent and I go for a look one Wednesday after work. It's a sublet and the owner's son shows me round. His dad is working abroad at the moment and is renting the one-bed fully furnished. The son seems stressed and is standing in the hallway the whole time and reluctantly takes off his shoes when I ask about the balcony. I know from the beginning that I'm not going to rent the apartment.

I take a detour on the way home and listen to music. The apartment is in an area with both houses and blocks of flats and there's also a Free Church on site but nothing else. You don't feel nature out here. It could be anywhere, but it's here.

I decide to stay with Mona.

The first time we drive out on the ice, I don't notice. We're out driving one evening as usual when I'm up visiting him and after a while I realise that we are not on a road any more. Not a road with asphalt or gravel or different lanes. It's late and I might have dozed off.

I know that he does this, drives on the ice, but it's always seemed so distant and I have always tried to get him to understand that I never wanted to do it. He hasn't said anything now. There is snow on the ice all round us, we are driving on a ploughed track, this is a common pleasure. Occasionally he skids and I grip carefully the handle on the side of the seat and hold tightly.

I say nothing.

13

I go home with Stina after work, she's going to lend me her driving test theory book. I've been here once before at a party and a few times in connection with Hotel-Saturdays. The door is unlocked and there's noise coming from inside the apartment. The sound of people talking and beer cans against a table top. Kalle and someone whose name I can't remember are sitting on the small sofa with their shoes and coats on and each with a can of beer in their hand. Stina doesn't seem to immediately notice them and I wonder whether either of them actually lives here, but when I look around and remember how small the flat is, I also remember that Stina lives here alone. And then I remember that Jenny has said before in the car on the way to the Hotel that Stina's apartment is like a youth club. That there are always people hanging out there, even if she's not home herself.

The table in front of the sofa is covered in beer cans which rattle about as soon as one of the guys on the sofa laughs or changes position. One of the table's legs is held together with tape and is slightly wonky. Under the table there's a stack of pizza boxes. Stina shouts out from the bedroom alcove that she thinks she's found the book.

It isn't quiet here, not always but it can be quiet in a way like nowhere else I know. Usually there is someone driving a car here, close by, or further away, just passing by on the road that leads to Norway, or to the coast. A dog barking somewhere. But there is a fundamental silence here. When it's quiet, it is perfectly quiet. No humming, nothing in the distance. To start with, it fascinated me, before I got used to it. But this silence will never be comforting.

I'm sitting in the stockroom, adding sale prices into the system. In other stores, the special offer prices are automatically uploaded to the system every week, but here and in some of the other small shops, we don't have the latest technology. On the next screen is the feed from the CCTV cameras. It's just as interesting to see how people move about the shop as it is to see what they end up buying. There are those who systematically walk down the aisles and never go back on themselves, I guess that their shopping lists must be equally systematic, the goods listed in the order in which you come across them in the shop. Then there are those who move with intent towards a specific item only to later wander, confused, back for something they have forgotten or missed.

 His gait does not stand out in any particular way but I recognise him immediately, even though the picture quality is not great. It's Friday and he should be sitting in an auditorium at the university, but he's now suddenly there amongst the packs of pasta and trying to choose one together with a girl. Even though I know that he always prefers gnocchi, I finally see him pick out a long packet – spaghetti.

He calls later that day: I'm home, just so you know.

Hands over to me. Waits for me to say something about meeting, or to change subject. I don't take over, let the conversation stall, not an uncomfortable silence, not awkward, but unbearable. He finishes without having said a word about the girl he has brought home with him.

It's unusual to not have a direction, to not be able to see a horizon. I am not headed anywhere.

14

The curiosity as to what I am doing here is a collective interest. One can ask at the till in the shop, but once a few people have found out why I am here, the questions cease. It's enough that a few have asked, now everyone knows the answer.

But of course they still don't know. They cannot know, because I don't know. There's not a clear answer anymore.

Stina invites me to a party at her place one Friday, she asks me at lunch, Fredrik and Laila are also sitting at the table and at first it's not clear who she is asking, as we have just been discussing the fact that there won't be enough discounted mince, or at least everyone else has just been discussing this. Instead, I've been wondering whether it would be obviously visible that I'm not at all involved in what's happening at the table.

Then Stina suddenly says that she's holding a party. I understand that she is not saying this to Laila, I know that they never see one another outside of work, but I assume that she's addressing Fredrik, even if I've never seen them together outside of work either. And I finally nod, when I meet her eyes and say that it sounds fun.

The darkness never bothers me. When I was getting ready to move, people asked me about the darkness, how I have prepared myself for it, if I had a huge supply of lamps in my suitcases or if I'd been guzzling vitamin D. I hadn't thought about it. I knew it would get dark here. And that it stays that way for a long time, but it just was not a concern. And it hasn't been. More the opposite, a kind of comfort. It's like a warm room, the darkness. With walls which curl around me and shut out everything else.

I'm not affected by the dark in the way that everyone thought I would be. I don't need light therapy, or any other kind of therapy for that sake.

I am standing alone in the village square and it's seven o'clock. From the lawn next to the church a sort of summer haze rises and the air is crisp. The bus swings in front of me and the tyres rasp against the damp cobbles.

Everyone drives if they want to get away from here, but I take the bus the morning that I decide to go. It's the last day of my holiday and I take a bus to the coast. My backpack sits on the seat next to me. We barely make it out of the village before I fall asleep.

I don't know what I was thinking or what I was planning on doing when I arrived. I wander aimlessly around the town centre amongst the shops and restaurants. I'm not used to all these people, who barely look at you or stop to see who you are or say hello.

I decide to go to the cinema and buy a ticket for a film I've never heard of. The theatre is almost empty, as it's in the middle of the day and it is summer. The film is Finnish and is about a man who loses his memory and by the time it's over I've forgotten that it is daytime. Out on the street it's warm and light and it stings my eyes.

15

It feels almost excessive to go to a hotel, and strange. I have never stayed in a hotel alone, never paid to sleep in a hotel. It is expensive, I check the prices before I finally decide, but I do decide. I had forgotten to check when the last bus went and now I have to spend the night at the coast.

Most of the others in the hotel lobby are in suits and have small, hard suitcases, so I stand out with my rucksack as my only luggage, but no one notices this apart from me.

The bed is large for a single and the sheets are neat and white. The air conditioning is on and produces a muffled hum in the background. I sleep in my t-shirt, freshly showered but with unbrushed teeth.

I don't remember having seen cold like this before I came here. Cold that sits in the skin and in the hair, paints your hair white, grey with small crystals of ice. A cold that makes everything move a little more slowly and makes everything a little clearer. A cold that is visible, when you know what to look for.

The driving school teacher says that it is important both to look in the rear view mirror and to turn around. He says something about a blind spot and how one sees objects as nearer and further away in the mirrors. I reverse carefully around the corner then drive forwards again. First he looks satisfied but then he nods towards the gearstick: You need to brave getting up past second gear on a stretch like this.

It was so hard for me to imagine the place when I first met him and had not been here. I had never been anywhere like it, never long enough that it registered at least. Never long enough that I'd have been able to imagine how this village looked. How small it was, but still sufficient. And how big everything else was, the surrounding nature.

He told me about the two streets that were the centre of the community. First the main road and then within that, the two streets. The one with the grocery shop, where there was also a pizzeria, the one with the pub in the basement. Where Olle's was too and a number of houses and an electronics store and a furniture shop. And then there was the other street, with the pharmacy, off license, the two hair dressers, the clothes store and the photographer. The streets which met at the square where the buses went from, where the church and the museum were. And then the main road which led on out to the schools and the leisure centre with the swimming pool and the library and on to the cemetery if you went right, but to the Hotel if you went left, up the hill. Compact and small, but still bigger than

I had imagined.

And how the whole village has become something else. How my walks and all the trips home from the Hotel have changed the distances and made the streets different. How that which was his ceased to be his. How it still did not become mine.

16

There is only an ice compartment in my little kitchen, but Mona lets me use part of her large freezer in the basement. The first months here, I don't buy any frozen food, only stuff that I'll use the same day. Then, later, I suddenly forget about that and buy a large bag of frozen broccoli that's on sale. Mona has marked a section of the freezer with my name and left it empty. On her side, there are what I think are several parts of an elk. This is the kind of freezer one has up here. Big enough to hold the results of a hunting trip. I don't really know why I had not wanted to use the large freezer, Mona had been offering it to me since I moved in, but it still feels in some way like I am an intruder in her house, even though I'm paying rent. Sometimes I have the same feeling outside of home. I'm a foreign power that has arrived here unbidden.

Lena gets me up to speed on most things and she tells me a lot without being directly asked. About where to take road trips, about nature walks, about which time of day and the year it is best to go skiing and other things I don't know. She'd tell me more if I asked, I'm sure of it, but I've never been one to ask too many questions. I'm more of a listener. But I still learn plenty during the first months here. Take in most of what I hear. But I also realise that things will remain blurred before I understand all the connections. And before I've experienced it all. And that I'll never catch up with those who have always lived here.

I should have positioned myself clearly. It is Stina's party and two guys who usually hang out with Kalle have started asking me about which is better, here or there, here or where I lived before. I should have clearly chosen a side; I can see this on them. I try to just avoid the question and it isn't so hard, given that they answer their own questions. I've just not ever thought about it, never made the comparison. There is nothing to compare, they are such vastly different places, different feelings, different full stop.

Spring never comes here, so this year I miss spring for the first time. After winter there is a short pre-summer or springwinter but no spring. I miss the spring flowers, I notice to my surprise. Flowers have never been especially important to me.

He and I no longer see one another so often and our conversations have turned to small talk for the time being. At work it mainly consists of gossip and banter. At home I am silent. Of course I still speak to Mona when we occasionally meet in the common spaces of the house, but otherwise I am quiet.

I do not have a radio at home, but I get in the

habit of turning the TV on as soon as I get in from work. The noise of the TV becomes a comfort to me, a home of sound. I've almost entirely stopped listening to music. My CDs are gathering dust on one of the two shelves I've put up on the pale grey wall. There are two windows in the large room. In front of one of them hangs a brown and floral blind, probably from the sixties. The other window has a more modern variant. They are both Mona's and were there when I arrived. The décor is still Spartan, even though I've now been here for several months. As well as the shelves and the bed with the new nightstand, there is a small kitchen area in the large room. It consists of two hotplates and a sink and a little fridge. In the hall is an abandoned writing desk and a straining chest of drawers.

17

That second when he climbs out of the car that he's borrowed from a friend. A large car which will fit everything I own and take me to my new home. That moment we waited for and which is becoming something else. The second when he gets out of the car and our looks say something else, we know that this is the beginning of something, but the end. Above all, the end.

We have planned it as a new beginning, this is when we start for real. I move up there, leaving that which was my home and will call home that which is his. And we'll be together more. Properly. Full time.

He drives down to me, starts out much later than he had planned, but it's no problem for him. He is used to driving, also in the dark and where he comes from, everyone drives. Drives a lot. And the car he has borrowed has extra lights so winter and darkness are never a problem. And when he arrives I've finished packing and carrying everything outside and said goodbye, because we need to head straight off. And our eyes meet the second he gets out of the car and that which becomes the beginning becomes the end. But we

61

pack my things and then he sleeps for an hour, drinks a cup of coffee and then we go. Towards an ending which also becomes a beginning.

I pass my test. It's October when I pass and suddenly I have a temporary driving license in my hand. Winter waits in the air and I've never driven on snow, but now I can drive according to the piece of paper.

Maria also passes and gives me a hug as if in triumph even though we are don't know one another. She is of course much younger than me, but that's no hindrance to friendship here. You can't be so fussy.

Maria is friends with all the people I don't know. She hasn't worked at it, it's just happened. I haven't worked at it either.

18

There's a stuffed bear in the basement at the Hotel.
Stina shows it to me one Saturday night when she's
drunk. The music is loud and we are on our way to
the toilets. She's holding my arm. Before we get to the
toilets, she suddenly swings out to the left and takes
me down to the basement. They don't normally open
down here, it's not intended that you go down here,
but it's not locked either and suddenly we're in a room
with leather armchairs and an open fire. This is where
the bear is. It's standing on its back legs with its paws
up ready to attack or defend. Its teeth are bared and
glinting in the dim light from the floor lamps which are
placed around the room.

Just as quickly as we came in, we're on our way
out again. Stina says nothing but pulls me back up and
on the stairs the thudding becomes loud music again.

At some point before I move here, some point before
I meet him, I see this place on TV. I can't remember
what the point of the documentary is, but it takes place
in the village and without getting into what it's about, I
think the place seems sleepy. The idea of living there is

63

unthinkable to me. Living here. I don't think that back then. There is no alternative because I don't need an alternative.

I think that the place is sleepy and I have never heard the name before. It's on a sign on the TV, the one you see when you drive into the village. First the name in Swedish and then underneath in Sami. A new place for me. Not a place to remember.

When I met him and get to see his home for the first time, I've forgotten the documentary. But when he drives me there from the airport in the neighbouring town, when we drive into the village, I recognise the sign.

It isn't sleepy here. Out in the surrounding nature it is perhaps quiet and it's clearly far from stressful here but not sleepy.

When it snows at night I'm almost always woken up early by the snowploughs. Fredrik tells me that the guys ploughing at night get paid more and are therefore attentive to whether it's snowing and are happy to get out and work unsociable hours. The morning after it's snowed the drifts are both harder and softer. Hard edges that attest to the ploughs' progress, with an eiderdown cover.

The drifts can be a metre high here. Metre high walls that eat up sound and light.

19

In winter you cruise about on your snow scooter. The same thing as with a car, just driving round aimlessly, but with a scooter the possibilities are greater. Scooter trails exist but there are also frozen lakes. Nature is wide open. You can go wherever you like and because of exactly that, also nowhere at all. I've never ridden a scooter. Fredrik looks at me for a long time when he hears this during a *fika* break and after a moment he laughs: Sometimes I forget that you're not from round here.

And I almost manage to answer something before he adds: Ha, I'm just kidding.

Everyone laughs. Including me, of course.

I don't think much about my age; it's getting rubbed out here. When Lena invites me over for dinner one day it makes me think that she could have been my mum and her two sons who are sat at the table at dinner are closer to my age than she is, but here it doesn't matter.

Occasionally someone asks if I don't miss one thing or another. Cinema or cafés or shops or concerts. But they don't exist in this life. Not here. It's too far away to miss. There's no point comparing. And I've never taken with me thoughts of that which I left behind. Not things, not people, not places, not feelings. I'm here now and everything here began here. From scratch.

I usually answer that I miss it sometimes.

20

He's home and it's almost a year since I moved here. He called first and comes to pick me up in his small, but fast car. I'm wearing ski pants and warm shoes and the winter coat I got from Lena. The engine's idling and he looks up from the light of his mobile when I come out of the house. We drive round the village and he tells me about university and the coast and the cold and then lastly about her. Her name is Emelie and she is taking the same course as him. He looks happy but I know that he's trying to hide it.

We drive out on the ice and it's uncomfortable even though I know that the ice must be at least a metre thick by now. He tries to calm me down as usual: It's safer driving here than on the roads.

We drive and talk and then we're quiet because we still can be with one another. The time we spent getting to know each other was a long time.

I have a job to go to and I have free days. I don't have much else but I don't get bored. Bored would be the wrong word.

At the start I just have a small piece of paper to confirm that I have the right to drive a car. Later I get a letter about ordering my actual license. I don't have any recently taken photos so I go down to the village photographer. He shares an office with the journalist who writes in the local paper. In the window there are photos of students and married couples and babies and I remember suddenly how I actually brought my student cap here with me when I moved. I took everything with me. It just feels so remote now. The other and previous.

The photographer is out buying lunch, the journalist tells me when I go into the office and the small bell over the door rings. She says that I'm welcome to sit and wait and points to a worn out leather sofa inside the lilac painted door.

A few minutes later the photographer comes in. The journalist from the local paper nods towards me and the photographer smiles in recognition: You from the grocery store, a photo for your driving license, right?

21

There is no later. Just tomorrow and maybe next week, but I don't look further ahead. I don't know what I should look for.

When I started working at the shop, there were several people who said they could sense on me that I came from a city, that I was stressed, rushed things. Thought about later the whole time and never about now.

Now it's just now. No later beyond next week, if that. I even think I'm walking more slowly. My walks are saunters.

After a week of having a driving license I decide to buy a car. People here have a car. During the lunchbreak I look through the classified ads in the paper and I feel Fredrik's gaze when I'm looking under Cars For Sale: So, it's time to get a car now?

And I hear how he smiles when he says it, as if he has been waiting for this. I look up at him and say that none of the adverts were from here and then he tells me that his sister is selling her car, a small and old car that he thinks might suit me.

It's an unusually warm day, but there is still snow on the ground in places. Fredrik drives me to a bungalow near the school. He has insisted on driving and coming along even though I said it would take fifteen minutes to walk or five to cycle. I've never met his sister, but I recognise her of course when I see her. I recognise everyone who buys groceries. Her name is Anna and she's moving away and seems to think that the car should stay here. Fredrik says that you should buy a car from the inlands and not the coast because they grit the roads there in winter and it rusts the cars. The car is green but clearly faded and looks quite boxy. It's really old and has a choke to start the engine.

Most people who live here were born here, the others have had to give their explanations. You don't just come here and you don't just blend in.

Leaving here doesn't require an explanation.

22

At some point in the beginning when he and I were together I was also as sick as this. I asked him to ring as soon as he got home from school and then our conversation carried on the whole evening, for several hours, every evening. Some of the days my throat hurt too much to speak and I let him understand that he should keep talking. Recount. That was when I got to know him, and got to know the place that's now my home. I say home about this place. I was careful to do so already from the start, but now it's stopped feeling forced to call it that.

The yoghurt runs out on the first day. That's the only thing I can stand to eat. My throat is thick, my nose blocked and I have a fever. My pyjamas are too warm one minute and too cold the next. My hair sticks to my cheeks when I wake up, hungry, after a sweaty dream. I eat the yoghurt as it is, still manage to pour it into a bowl. By evening it's finished. Me too.

During the night it gets better. As if the fever has gone down and it doesn't hurt as badly everywhere. But it's just dreams and sleep, I realise in the morning.

Skin a hypersensitive outer layer, pyjamas

fabric like sandpaper.

Everything around me cold, me warm. Hot. I eat the fruit and vegetables that I have at home. Four carrots, two apples, half a cucumber. A banana. Try to drink plenty of water, but don't manage.

The third day the food has really run out. Given where I work, I never do a big shop, rather every other day. On a shelf I find a can of chickpeas which I eat as they are. They are filling and last almost the whole day. The fever goes up and down. My throat hurts constantly.

It's been so long since I was this sick, I think between fits of shivering. Several of my colleagues have had some sort of influenza and I guess I must have the same thing. I've heard Laila describe her fever somewhere on the perimeter of my thoughts one lunchbreak. Everything becomes a project. Going to the toilet. Making more tea. Finding something to eat. Today it's chopped tomatoes. With a few spices it tastes almost like cold tomato sauce. I have a bit of pasta in the house but can't be bothered to cook it.

Right at the back of the shelves I find some porridge oats, almost a half bag. It's the fifth day of fever, but it feels different today. As if I might actually get better. And after three more days, when I've almost finished the bag of oats, I go back to work.

23

There is nothing else. The place. The village and the surrounding nature which added together are the place. Those which for me are such different things, both almost exotic in the beginning and now whereas the village has almost become a kind of everyday the forest has not changed notably. It will never become commonplace, even if I think that I'll get used to it, that it will start to seem natural. Perhaps not even strange. It's still so new. It makes me think of a postcard when I'm out there. Trim the edges and put it in a frame. That's how I've seen this previously. With him as a guide. Like doing a tour of your own home. Easy to get blinded by the routine, hard to appreciate the uniqueness of the place. But he understood. Showed me those views. The postcard views.

Looked proudly at me, pointed toward the fell. Knew the name of the plants that actually thrive here.

The place as a unity of nature and village. Me as an observer.

Part two

24

Dark as the winter is here, the summer is just as light. I find it harder to get used to the light. I've never seen this light before, much less tried to sleep through it. Without my roller blinds it just wouldn't work. I pull them down early during the summer. Try to convince myself that it's dark and think about what time it actually is. The light, quiet nights are so different from everything else. If I forget the blinds, they creep up on me, the nights. The darkness doesn't affect me, not that I can feel, but the light. The light does.

At work we have blue vests on that show that we work here. They don't really have any sort of shape to them, even if there is a special women's version that everyone apart from Fredrik and the odd guys who work here part time have on. We are allowed to wear ordinary clothes under the vests, but my ordinary clothes also become a uniform. I can't be bothered deciding what to wear. The same jeans every day and a t-shirt, usually in black.

Most things are routine now. How my working days

look, going to Olle's on a Saturday and buying the same sweets and the same kind of magazines, either eating the sweets at home and staying in or going with Stina to the Hotel. What never becomes routine is when I work, the roster doesn't follow any particular pattern, I've said that it doesn't matter to me which days or which shifts I work, so I end up with an irregular timetable, shifts that run over. But my days off look almost always the same, regardless of when they fall. In winter I have sweatpants on all day, because if I go out I just put ski trousers on over the top. But mainly I'm home in my two rooms. Sleep later, stay in bed, sometimes actually watch something on the TV that's always on.

All routines can make time pass slowly, but even if the days and especially the evenings often feel slow, time goes by quickly. Days turn to weeks, to months. And years.

25

We are at the Hotel. I'm there with Stina and Kalle and someone called Jessica who I think is Kalle's cousin. It is of course Saturday and I don't know where the others are, I'm sat in an armchair next to the bar. A guy who I think is called Linus knocks back a shot at the bar and grabs a beer at the same time as he turns around and looks out across the room. I see in his gaze that he's looking for something and when he sees me it's as if he slows down. We've only just arrived at the Hotel and I know that it'll take a few hours before I get a lift back into the village again, but at the same time I want to be left in peace. Before the guy who I think is called Linus makes it over to my chair, I get up and go quickly over to the basement stairs. When I get downstairs I go straight to the bear room and sit down in an armchair opposite the bear. It's pretty quiet down here and nothing gives away what's happening one floor up. The bear scares me somehow, the way it stands with its paws ready to strike right across your face, but at the same time I can't stop myself going towards it and the bear's stance also gives me a sense of security.

I've been sitting with the bear for perhaps a half

hour when a drunk couple find their way into the room. I know immediately that I want to go home when they come in. I don't care where the others are but I still see Stina and Lars making out by the toilets when I go to get my jacket. A taxi isn't an option, as there are hardly any here.

It's dark, I'm not bothered by the cold anymore, it's part of the place, as is the darkness, but I'm used to being in the village when it's dark and there are lights there. I press a button on my mobile phone every time it dies and use its light to guide my way. It doesn't provide a sufficient light at all, but as soon as it goes off, all the snow and all the drifts and the forest next to them go black and with the light from the screen they become a grainy dark grey. It's two hours until the Hotel closes and no one is driving home at this time, but every now and then a car drives up the hill and I'm glad that I have reflectors on my clothes. As I'm getting closer to the crossroads at the bottom of the hill I'm able to see better as there are streetlights down there. Just when I know I've made it down, I drop my phone and in the half-darkness I can't see at all where it has landed. I crouch down at the side of the road and feel my way forward with my mittens. Eventually I give up and get up to go home but just then I catch the phone with my foot and it ends in the road, visible and I can gather it up. It's covered in snow and won't turn on again.

26

I buy a new phone. For some peculiar reason, an electronics store manages to stay in business here therefore I only need to walk a few streets away to buy a mobile. I've managed two days without it, hoping that no one would ring at the same time as wanting someone to do so. The phone numbers don't move over with the SIM card, so when I get my new clean phone working I don't have anyone's number. I know the family's number by heart, as well as his, even if I haven't called him for a very long time. Some of my old friends' numbers I remember too, but when I get to eleven numbers, including the one for work which I find in an old paper I have at home, then that's that.

I play a game that's installed on the phone and then put it down on the table.

The forest's framing of the village. The village which is barely visible from a plane, this is nature's domain.

A new guy starts at work. He's called Finn and works mainly weekends and occasionally after school, he goes to the college in the village, but lives in another town.

He's naturally very quiet but great with customers.

It's Saturday and Finn is standing behind me at the till to learn. I say hi to the customers, so does he, I tell them the total and how much their change is if they're paying cash, but otherwise it's fairly quiet except the beep when I scan the barcodes, and the humming of the checkout belt. The silence becomes even more apparent when I'm replaced at the till and go on my *fika* break, Finn comes with me and as it's the weekend there aren't that many of us working and it's just us two on a break right now. I feel that Finn expects that I will lead the conversation. But now we're sitting there, opposite one another at the oval table, I realise that I've never really begun a conversation here.

I try to remember to clip my fingernails regularly, barely let them grow more than a few millimetres, but sometimes I forget and then they break immediately. Usually at work, it's mainly there that I'm doing things with my hands. Sometimes I catch them on something, other times I don't even need to do that for them to break.

27

The blood is sticky, that's how I know that it's blood. It's dark in the room and I'm lying on my bed looking at the ceiling, following the strip of light from the gap in the roller blinds with my eye. Feel that it's running from my nose, wipe it with my hand. I get up and feel my way with the clean hand to the door, open it and go out into the corridor that leads to the bathroom with the pink porcelain. Hand under my nose, I turn on the light and stand by the sink. Look at myself in the mirror, see how it keeps running, slowly from my left nostril. I clean myself up and sit down on the toilet, lean my head back and sit there until it stops. I see that the clock in the corridor shows one thirty when I turn out the bathroom light and find my way back to bed.

Even though I'm not the most experienced in the shop, it falls to me to teach Finn all the routines. Given he just works part time, it takes a few weeks before I've managed to show him everything. We hardly talk, instead he walks round the shop with me and watches what I'm doing. I do everything a bit slower and after a while he starts to do the same things.

When his summer holidays are approaching I've taught him everything and one afternoon we're changing the price labels on jams together. The jam is going to be a few öre more expensive. We work methodically and, without really having agreed on it, I'm the one ripping the old labels off and he's putting the new prices in place on the edge of the shelf.

When it's almost closing time, Marie comes over to the dry goods shelf where we're standing and says that Finn's mum had to go to the vet with their dog and so she can't pick him up. Finn looks worried but doesn't say anything. We have two prices left to change and when we're done I turn to him: Do you want me to give you a lift home?

It's the first time I drive outside of the village and the immediate surroundings, but I know which direction I'm going in. To start with there's just one road and when after twenty minutes we're getting closer Finn breaks the silence and tells me which tracks I need to turn in to and where I need to go straight ahead. There was a quarry here, but the only thing left is the quarry building that we drive by at a distance. The high building feels misplaced in the empty landscape.

Precisely because all options are open and I can go wherever I like, it feels like the exact opposite.

28

I'm eating a purple plum on my coffee break. Fredrik stands at the counter with a crispbread with anchovies in his hand and Marie and Laila are sitting at the table. I put the pit on a piece of kitchen roll in front of me. Shift the paper back and forth with my finger and half listen to the conversation about a coming weekend, that's being held around the table.

Twice a year there's a market, it's not unique to the village and moves from place to place but it always bears the mark of its surroundings. The village expands during market week. Fills with excited anticipation and former residents who make their way back home. I never feel so foreign as I do then.

It's exactly that time now, it's Wednesday and already a week earlier there was nothing to talk about other than the market. There are many rituals around it and everyone knows them inside out, even me. Even on Market Saturday the Hotel is still a focus, but already on the Thursday people start going out. The pub one day, the other hotel the next day and then the Hotel. With additional expectations.

And when Saturday comes, there are of course

more people at the Hotel. Otherwise it's pretty much like usual except there's a band playing and a DJ in the basement. In the bear room. The bear is moved a bit to the side to make place for the DJ's decks but I can see its eyes flashing with reflections from the disco ball. It suddenly looks lonely, in this glitzy light, with all the people dancing around it.

It's unimportant that most of the things that happen happen exactly like any other Saturday, because it's by definition a special Saturday. And people have dressed accordingly, spent a bit more time getting ready before coming out, started drinking a bit earlier in the evening.

This is one of those nights where no one wants to be the driver.

I like taking a shower after work, before deciding what, or if, I'll eat. I like standing in the pink bathtub and feeling how the water runs down my body. It's not every day that I can be bothered to shower, sometimes I go straight to the fridge or the bed which is still a sofa at that point. Sometimes end up falling asleep there. With the washing up next to me, still dressed. Sometimes I wake up in the night and go quietly to the toilet and brush my teeth.

Sometimes I don't sleep at all.

Before I moved here I only hung out with people born the same year as me.

When Finn starts working at the shop and goes on summer holiday from school it suddenly strikes me that we're actually a similar age.

29

Sometimes I wake up at night and it feels like I haven't slept at all. In winter I look up at the completely dark ceiling and try to see the edges of the walls and roof, my lamp in the middle of the room, my hand in front of my face. Only when I look at the window can I see anything. In the gap between the blind and the window there is a hint of streetlight and after a while contours appear. I never look at the clock when I wake up. Try not to think. Fend away thoughts that I can't deal with. Everything feels much harder at night, heavy thoughts are heavier, the darkness darker. But then the alarm finally goes and I must have slept.

Stina and I make room for the Christmas hams in one of the fridges. They take up a lot of space and we have to move lots of other goods. It's Monday and Stina seems to have been drinking on the Sunday. She's not her usual self, more like the Sunday version which is not that unusual. We get the heavy hams down one by one from the cart they came in with the refrigerated truck this morning. I go to get the sign with the price and just as I come into the storeroom I hear that Stina has dropped a Christmas ham on the stone floor. The sound clearly lets on that the ham's weight has caused the plastic to split. I go towards the cleaning cupboard instead.

No one falls through the ice here, because they know the ice here. And because the ice is thick here.

I don't know anything about the ice. The thickness in centimetres doesn't mean anything to me. When can you stand on ice? Does it need to be a metre thick or ten centimetres? I don't know when ice breaks up or why.

30

Sometimes on Saturdays Kalle's car doesn't pull up outside Mona's house and I'm still sitting in my bed in knitted socks and with my hand in the bag of sweets.

It's a Sunday when just Finn and I are working when we start to talk to one another. It's after I drove him home to his town for the first time and after I've taught him everything about the shop. And we don't begin to speak that much, but we at least say something other than just the bare minimum.

Finn has been so quiet during the time that we have worked together, since he started at the shop. And I don't know much about anyone here, but I know even less about Finn.

He works extra to earn money for taking his driving test, he says, and then he leaves the storeroom and goes out into the shop: I'll fill up the *karra!*

He comes back in through the stockroom doors when I don't answer: Maybe you don't know what that is.

And then he laughs, in a kind way: Sweets, perhaps you call them.

We both laugh.

When everything is finished and it's twelve o'clock, we open the shop for the day, for the four hours it's open on Sundays. We take turns to sit at the till, max one hour at a time and stack the shelves and take it easy in the stockroom.

It feels as if my veins have become more visible. They stick out more from under my skin, which has always been pale, but seems even paler now. When I take my jeans off to get in the shower, I have a large bruise on the side of my thigh. After thinking for a moment, I remember banging into the freezer when I was unpacking goods. It changes from purple to yellow in some places and I have never had such a large bruise before. The skin feels warm when I touch it.

31

There is one week to go until midsummer and I take the car over to the neighbouring town to see if I can find a pair of sandals. It's not really summer yet, but there's talk of it getting really warm and I realise that I don't really have any shoes that would suit that kind of summer. On the way back, with a bag from the shoe shop on the passenger seat, I realise how conscious I've become of the sound of the engine. Something sounds wrong. For a moment I consider stopping the car but there is nothing here, aside from the forest, so I drive home and hope that nothing will come of it.

After parking in the drive, behind Mona's car which she doesn't use, I get out to take a look at the car, but give up before I even open the bonnet. I don't know what I'm looking for and wouldn't know what to do if I found it.

The next day, on my *fika* break, I ask Fredrik if he can help me with the car and he says he'll happily take a look.

I make it home and have dinner, a stew, before he knocks on the door: Did someone break in?

I smile, but it looks like he's still wondering

about it and I look around.

I've not really thought about how this place looks. How it started to look. How it has become. The wardrobe where my clothes should be but which stands there with its doors open and clothes streaming out over the floor, almost trying to escape. When you stand here, it actually looks as if someone has thrown them about but I know that's not the case, that it has just happened. From here you can see that there actually are places for everything but that nothing is in them. There could easily have been someone here, looking for valuables and rooting around, not leaving anything in the place where it came from. I can see that now and I quickly put on a pair of shoes so we can go outside.

Fredrik backs her car out of the drive. It's almost eight o'clock but it doesn't get dark now, just a slight dusk, later. He goes out and looks at the car and says he's pretty sure he's found the problem, that there is oil leaking from the gearbox.

A week later he's fixed the car and it sounds like it's supposed to again.

32

It's always evening. It's always that time of the evening when I'm making tea and actually watching the TV that's eternally on. I don't get stressed here, but the tempo in the evenings is even calmer. There is nothing lying ahead.

I don't think so much about how the day has been as I do about the simple fact that it's evening again. Sometimes I feel my stomach tighten, as if in realisation that time is actually passing quickly. Other times its more of a bland observation.

It's evening now, a summer evening and I've just pulled the blinds down to try and become tired but the light's presence is too insistent and I choose a chamomile tea and hope it will help.

Thoughts linger. Today becomes a day which becomes every day and the evening is constant. An evening without end with the light finding its way in behind the blinds and reminding me of the latitude. But normally I fall asleep eventually.

We each get a gift pack with shower gel and moisturiser from work at the start of the holidays. Fredrik gets a similar thing but in black. I never normally use body lotion, but after I shower that evening I sit down on the bed and open the bottle. A synthetic peach smell hits me as I rub the cream into my legs.

Before I meet him, before being familiar with this place or even knowing its name, I think this part of the country must be forest and mountains and wolves and bears. I'm young and a certain level of naivety is to be expected. The fact is that I've never given this part of the country a thought before, but now I know that, were I to do so, those are the things I would think of. But I don't. I'm unbothered and uninterested and have too much else to think about.

33

I am only attached to him here. No one else is connected to me, not him either, anymore. All the others here know each other in a wider sense. Know who the mum is, the cousin, the brother. Know who has been whose teacher and who has slept with who.

It's new for me, driving without a purpose. Driving round the village, on the ice, out on the backroads sometimes, without deciding where. And that you can drive over to someone's house without calling them first. Open the door and go in and shout hi. Even if I wanted to embrace this way of life, I don't know how. Not having a where, being completely plan free. And I don't have anyone to whose home I could drive over and go in. Maybe Stina wouldn't raise her eyebrows so much but I'd never feel comfortable.

At the same time as the interest in me wanes, I also lose interest in myself.

I make the bed with clean sheets and take a long shower in the pink bathtub in the bathroom which I share with

Mona. It's evening again and I'll soon be making tea and sitting up in the freshly made bed. I close my eyes in the shower and imagine my feet in the recently cleaned sheets. The window has been open all afternoon and evening and the scent of summer surrounds me when I come back to my room.

34

One way of getting away from here is to start studying. But April passes, as well as the last application day, without it crossing my mind. I have no future in mind. Either.

There's a pizzeria here but I've never eaten there until one Saturday when Stina rings in the evening and asks if I want to go there with them and eat before the Hotel. I guess it's her, Kalle and Jenny. It's the second time she's called me.

The others go for pizza number forty-nine and I do the same. I pick off the bits of ham on it, eat the pineapple but leave the crusts.

There's no breeze, as is often the case here. The difference is most obvious when you get to the coast and there's wind almost all the time. The contrast. The air feels warm, I'm bare legged in the shade on a jetty at the lake. There's a boat here, but I've never seen anyone use it. At the same time, I know that no one has just left it there, it would never have survived the ice.

There's another boat out on the lake, the lake

which is the closest you get to a sea here. Which feels as big as an ocean occasionally but which always reveals land and gives itself away.

I hold out as long as I can with the washing up. Or I wash up when it becomes necessary. After a few days the forks run out, but spoons do the job. Then they run out and I have to wash up. It takes a whole evening and the TV is on in the background. There's a nature documentary on. The presenter and some experts are looking for a bear, or signs of a bear. I turn towards the TV at the same time as I'm rinsing the plates. They find a bear in the end. They actually see it from a distance, but it's sufficiently close to make me shiver. The bear at the Hotel is one thing, living bears are something else. The program hasn't been filmed in this area, luckily.

For a long time, I think about the move as an expression of freedom. That it was not so much about getting free of something, just about becoming free. Moving out of home, having my own place. Living with my things, my sounds, my movements.

It's Thursday morning and I need to go to work soon. I've devoted the time since I got up to nothing at all. That's when I start thinking about freedom. My rhythm. My decisions. But actually no freedom.

35

In the space between the oven and the wall there are signs that I occasionally cook.

It's Monday and there are deliveries coming into the shop. The frozen goods need dealt with first, we put on gloves and those that have to go into the walk-in freezer put on one of the fleece tops that are hanging outside on hooks. All the new goods go furthest in and back because the older stuff has to get sold first. It gets cold even with the gloves.

Finn has started lessons at the driving school, he tells me when I'm giving him a lift home after work. He's on summer holiday from school and works much more now and I've given him a ride home several times. His salary will pay for the driving license, but it won't be as expensive as mine, nobody's is here. Most of them can do it all before they start taking lessons, most of them have been driving on the ice since they could reach the pedals. His birthday is in a month; if he's passed the theory test he'll take the practical the day after his birthday. He's already bought a car, when we get to his driveway he points at a small red car. Much newer than mine, but still old. He smiles, looks expectant.

Much of what I've left behind physically through moving here, I've also left behind psychologically. Not necessarily intentionally, and I've not thought about it so much either, but now and then I'm reminded of my old life. It's not that I miss it, more that I miss a now. A context.

I don't know what's caused my headache. If it even is a headache, but something hurts anyway.

It takes a while before I get used to the language, the dialect and the vocabulary. His way of talking that was the most beautiful thing in the world when we met. All our phone conversations that were always about something, about everything but which hardly needed to be because his voice was enough. Unique in the place where I lived before, but which was just a part of the community here. I'm sitting in bed with the TV on but flicking through the phone book and stop at his name. Such little significance now, compared with before. His name on the phone display before, his voice in my ear. His words in me. And later the ordinariness of his dialect here. That everyone speaks like that, everyone uses his words and expressions, the private becomes public but at the same time unintelligible from the mouths of others. That taking off can mean walking round the block but sounds so much more than that. Like getting into a car and driving for a while, at least a half hour, and it can also mean that. The almost silent affirmative answers that from him were so clear, but from others aren't at all, the customers in the shop who look at me again to make sure I've understood them. Because they know who I am and always know what I'm saying because they've heard it on the radio, the TV and all over, but I'd only heard him before I came here.

36

I come home from work and I leave my boots as near the door as I can, on the small doormat. They're damp and gritty, winter is losing its grip. My jacket I leave on one of my two chairs. The hook where it should hang has fallen down. I think about it every time I come home and take the jacket off, but the hook is still lying on a shelf, it'll soon be a year since it fell down.

My life takes up no space. Everything I brought with me fit into a car. It wouldn't do so now, but there's still not much that I own. I wonder where I'd move to if I were to leave and what I'd leave behind to get everything in one car. There's no straightforward answer. I can't move back. I knew that already when I left. Not so much because I left something as because I made a decision. I chose to leave and I made a choice when I stayed here even though we broke up and the two decisions mean that I won't change. It would be a change, moving back.

   I want a reason to go somewhere, but I can't come up with anything when I think about it and that's why I stay here.

One Saturday it takes longer than usual to close up, the shop is full of Norwegians and they take their time, possibly unaware of the opening hours. Finally, Fredrik takes the microphone in the storeroom and shouts that we are shut now. The Norwegians start moving towards the till, they all move in the same pattern through the shop and from the till I have to shout to Fredrik and ask him to bring more loose tobacco.

When we've managed to close and tally up the till, there are just ten minutes until Olle's closes and I half run, even though it's only a hundred metres away. I want to have enough time to choose my sweets, even if I'll still buy the same thing as last week.

We say hi to one another these days, the guy who really is called Olof and I, but I'm conscious of the difference between the hi he reserves for the locals and the one he gives me. This particular Saturday, his hi sounds slightly different, as if he actually had noticed that I hadn't come and was wondering where I was. I manage to choose my sweets and magazine before the sign is brought in, and before five o'clock I'm turning the key in the lock to my door.

37

I know exactly what I'll find when I got to empty the truck. I'm the one who ordered the pasta and flour and jams this week and there are no surprises. There are no surprises and everything is as it should be. Lena is stood at the deli counter and is slicing chops. Laila is lining up bananas in neat rows, Fredrik carries in the soda and mineral water and beer because it's heavy. I put the new goods behind the old ones and then sit at the till for an hour. Marie has explained that we only get to spend one hour at a time at the till, she's the union rep. She has said that we shouldn't accept anything else but everyone knows that Sonia wouldn't try anything else either. She was the union representative before she became the boss and Marie took over.

At lunch I choose a new ready meal, a new ready meal is an event when you've eaten the others dozens of times before. I come into the breakroom and Fredrik just manages to notice me and turn to his paper but I just manage to see how he tightens his muscles and looks at his reflection in the window.

I start to know the names of most people here. Not

because I've said hello to them, but because everyone talks about everyone and it's impossible not to learn over time. But what I don't learn are their number plates, the sound of their cars, how and who they are related to, where they live. That knowledge would need me to take part in the conversation, would require more knowledge about engine sounds.

Mona has said that I don't need to buy my own hoover. She said it the first day I lived here, she came in to check that everything had gone well with the trip up, that I had everything. When I'd listed a few things I was missing, she stopped me immediately when I got to cleaning products and said that I shouldn't think about such things, everything I needed was in the cupboard just outside the door which led from my end of the landing to the rest of the house.

I often think about that hoover, but it takes a long time before I borrow if for the first time. I buy a dustpan and brush in the shop, before I start working there, and clean up the worst of the dust mites with that.

I'm occasionally incredibly tired. A tiredness that spreads out into the body, floods out all over. It suits me well that nobody is expecting anything from me, that I don't have anyone to report to. My evenings can be my walks and my TV watching and my sporadic baths and my silence. I get so tired that I don't even do anything. I go to bed early and usually sleep well but sometimes the tiredness takes hold of me.

Patchy memories of him. Blurred. Washed out.

It doesn't matter. But at the same time he's the only concrete thing here. Was.

38

I have never been to any of the taller mountains nearby, up on the fells. For me that nature is inaccessible. Not inaccessible like the nearby nature, in the sense that it does not open itself to me when I visit, but genuinely inaccessible, physically. I don't know when I would go, nor how far I'd have to go, what it involves. They're there like a permanent background. Almost always snow-capped, regardless of season. I get used to the snowy peaks as a backdrop to the village and as a constant reminder of where we are. Where I am. Unaffected by how many degrees the thermometer shows, there can be snow lying just there. It belongs here and is never scared away. It's hardy and doesn't give up.

The Arctic Circle is so close, but since I moved here I've not been north of it. He took me up there once, a short drive and we were there, north of the Arctic Circle and still nothing had changed. And we are so close now that it doesn't make a difference that it is at a different latitude. How the sun just dips in the summer, down and then up again, without it being noticeable. And the dark in the winter. And the snow on the fells.

It's as if the nights never end. The darkness eats me, the darkness that almost always feels so safe, but now threatening. It doesn't matter when I start work in the morning, it's always dark and dark when I get off.

It's one of those days when the lock on the shop door hardly gives. After I've taken off my double layer of gloves to enter the code and quickly put them on again I realise that the lock has frozen. It has to be under minus 30 for that to happen, according to the others. I haven't looked at the thermometer since I got here, I can just look out and see the cold, almost hear it through the glass. The key wiggles back and forth but not enough. Standing still is uncomfortable and I think that it would go quicker if I took my gloves off but I don't want to.

Sudden steps on the concrete stairs up to the loading area, it's Laila with her surefooted gait, not weighed down by the cold: Give me the key, I've got it.

She almost sounds annoyed, but I know that's not her style. And I think that it's the first time she has said something directly to me.

She gets the door open, leaves the key in the lock and walks purposefully towards the changing room where we each have our locker with our identical blue vests. When I come in she's already managed to get her vest on and her work shoes with the distinctive sound, short clicks that with her quick pace mean that you can hear it's her from a distance. Now she goes in to organise the shop and I know that although I'll do the same thing, we'll work in parallel and not together.

112

The timetable in the changing room shows that Finn is coming in soon too, but he's always a bit late.

Ten minutes before opening time I've done everything I need to and make sure the boxes from yesterday are crushed up. The box crusher is full and I empty it, open the side of the large metal machine and attach the strap which holds the crushed cardboard boxes down in a thick pile. I get the lifter and take it out into the loading area. When I open the lock and lift up the door with my back to reverse out, I suddenly remember the cold and that I've forgotten to put a vest on. Finn's standing out there smoking one of his hand rolled cigarettes. No hat but he still looks completely unaffected by the cold: I'll take that for you.

He nods towards the lifter and leaves the cigarette in his mouth. No gloves either. I go in again.

What was the plan? I can't remember what I, or we, had thought when I moved here. What we were going to do here and how long I was going to stay here. Live here.

Outside the window it's almost exactly the same as a year ago, when I moved here, snow that sprays up, a mist of snow that won't settle. I slept at his place the first night, we arrived late, almost early, and he didn't unpack anything from the car. We shared the bed and that was one of the last times we would do, we both knew it.

Him, another life, so distant now. How the day after we unpacked everything I owned, that all fit into a car, and how it gradually became a home. How he never became a part of it. Never left any mark on the new home. That's why this home also became something other than what I had expected my first home to be. I'd thought about it so long, made plans that came to nothing. But instead it became this and this became just mine.

39

It's only very rarely that I need to use the choke to get
my car started. On the whole it's been very reliable
apart from that time when Fredrik fixed the gearbox.

I don't use the car that much anyway. Drive
out to the forest and sometimes drive to the neighbouring town. If I'm going to the coast, I take the bus. I
don't know the towns out there and don't want to have
to parallel park. Want to find my way, want to avoid
feeling unsure. The coast is in many ways more like my
old life. Bigger towns, people whose faces and names I
don't know. There's a comfort in it, the anonymity, but
the longer I live in this place, the more its smallness feels
like a comfort. There is comfort in people now knowing
that the green car is mine, that it was Fredrik's sister's
before that.

I can't be bothered to cook; there's yoghurt in the fridge
that I pour into a bowl and take with me, along with
a spoon and a box of cornflakes, back to my room.
There's nothing on TV which suits me fine.

It's Saturday and I'm on closing at the shop. Fredrik's

scooping the cash up out of the till and I bring in the signs with the week's mince price and the discounts on toilet paper. I look away over towards the church, people dressed in black coming out and gathering on the gravel path out front. There is a funeral and I know that Fredrik should be there but couldn't switch his shift. Everyone is at that funeral, almost everyone.

I've not left anything behind. That's what I think. But I didn't seek out this place either. And yet this is where I am.

40

I'll never be part of what everything and everyone is here. I can feel it for example when I'm with Stina and Kalle and Jenny at the Hotel.

I can't get into it. It's not because I wasn't born here, there are some, for example, who didn't move here until they were in sixth form and they still managed to become a part of everything. It's something else.

Sometimes it becomes clear, physically clear, I stay in my corner because I don't know what I should say or do. But normally I'm in amongst the others, but quite silent.

It's a dull pain. I hadn't really thought about it before one day when I can't feel it anymore. It's in my neck I think, or back, but the next day, when it's made a return it might actually be throughout my whole body that I can feel it. All over, but not in any particular place. And not that strongly, but nagging, insistent. Through work I get the name of a naprapathy practitioner where we get a discount. Her practice is in an apartment block near the shop. I extend my lunch break and go there before heating up today's ready meal.

The practice isn't that clearly signposted, but I am also aware that it is not necessary here. Everyone knows where everything is, but I'm still learning new things, after almost a year and a half here. Next to the entrance is a small, handwritten note. Underneath the basement stairs there are three doors: one that looks like it leads to a fuse box or something similar, one that must go to the cellar storage and then the naprapath's door. Her name and a phone number on the door, that's all. I knock and open it and a woman with black, long hair turns round to me with a smile: Yes, you really do have a crooked back, don't you? I recognise her from the shop and assume she knows who I am but I introduce myself anyway.

I undress my top half and she studies my back for a moment before asking me to lie down on the bed. There's a towel lying across it, but it's still chilly somehow.

Stina sometimes talks about leaving. But with her it's obvious that it won't happen. She never talks about where, or what she would do. And it's par for the course to say that you are not happy here. She isn't alone in feeling a need to express her unhappiness, but there is a big difference between not being happy and wanting to do something about it.

There is a clothes store in the village. Clothes, shoes, makeup and a load of interior design stuff in the same place. It's summer and quite warm out and I don't have any clean t-shirts when I get up. I don't start work until midday, so I manage to get down to Karin's Boutique, as the store is called. It's happened before that I have needed to stock up when I didn't have any clean laundry, but then it was pants and socks and we have those at the shop. The woman at the till is a bit older than I am and is normally at the Hotel with Marie from the shop.

I've only peered into Karin's Boutique before, through the three display windows that face out towards the street. It's warm in here too and I'm sweating underneath my sweater, the one I randomly put on in my hunt for something thinner. Fairly quickly I find a simple, white t-shirt, more expensive than I would have usually gone for, but there isn't a choice here. There is a white t-shirt, if I want another one, I'll have to drive at least 100 kilometres.

41

One Sunday, Sonia's husband and her sister take over in the shop so that we can all do something together, outside of work. It's August, a day with bright skies and sunshine, a hint of the coming autumn in the air. We are supposed to have outdoors gear on and I've spent a long time wondering what in my wardrobe comes closest. Even Stina has waterproof trousers and a thin windbreaker. Everyone here knows how to dress appropriately, but my jeans and my thin cotton jacket still feel fine.

We are to meet at the shop at eight o'clock sharp, it's going to be a full day. When I get there, most of the others are already sitting the minibus. Stina arrives last, a quarter of an hour late, and I know that she has been out at the Hotel the night before. Because it was a Saturday yesterday and because she keeps her sunglasses on when she gets in the bus.

The bus journey takes forty-five minutes and outside the tinted windows are firs and pines and the road towards Norway. The bus at last swings in to a smaller road where it stops. We get out and Sonia takes the lead.

The landscape feels different in company. After him, I've only been out here alone. This nature has been my place, even though still not within my grasp. Today it feels as if I know this nature. I'm not so unconsciously conscious as some of the others, don't get it, don't know how it all fits together, but I am close to this nature.

We're standing at a picnic area with wooden shelter and a barbecue. The shelter is full of memories, names and years and declarations. Fredrik and Stina laugh at several of the carvings. Remember and imagine. I walk along the outside of the red-painted structure. Feel the wood under my hand, a splinter sticks but I get it out just as quickly.

On my free days, I sometimes wake up in bed and don't know what time it is. Don't know if I have just fallen asleep or if I need to go to work. When I eventually get the time right, know which side of the day I'm on, it still takes a long time before I feel properly awake. The dreams still hang around, the dizziness too.

It hits me that I have not touched another person since he was last home. Since he was last home and I knew about it and got a quick hug.

42

I've learnt to recognise certain signs and Finn is one of those who will leave. That he's bought a car is in this case not a sign that he'll stay. Maybe he'll head for the coast, perhaps further south than that.

Finn tells me about his plans for when he is finished at college. It's the end of the summer and he has his driving license. We finish at the same time and he asks if I want to go out for a bit in his car. We leave the village and somewhere along the road he stops. One of those places that some people know about. I don't.

It's a warmish evening, but autumn occasionally appears in the air. Finn rolls a cigarette and smiles when I grimace at it: It's really fucking nice here all the same.

And by the tone of his voice, I know that I was right; he's one of those who leave.

He takes a drag on the cigarette.

There are of course those who come back too, the revenants. But they are harder to see.

He's going to London, he tells me. With a friend from the coast who I've heard about by name before. He says friend, but I understand that they are a couple.

Or that they will be. They've met on the internet and a few times in person and I think it's him who has made Finn want to leave. That he has got Finn to understand that maybe he wants to try something else.

I don't often think about my breathing, that my breaths never feel whole, that they always feel interrupted. So long as I have something to do at work or I'm watching something on TV which I am actually watching, then I don't think about it. But then, as soon as I have some time, a break or a free day, it becomes an irritation. Not so that I get short of breath, but so that it feels the whole time like I will do.

Once a year there is an appraisal, I am told in the break room. Marie says that it's when you should ask about a pay rise, there's actually a kitty for it, even if we all have collectively agreed salaries. When it gets to Thursday and it's my turn, Sonia and I sit in the small room where the safety deposit box is, where we count the money. She asks me to tell her how I'm doing and how I think it's going and I answer how I think I'm doing. It's hard to put words on emotions, I feel. Difficult to explain my feelings for the job, to interpret them when I do feel something. It still takes an hour before we are done. I haven't said anything about a pay rise.

During the afternoon *fika*, when those who smoke leave the break room, Fredrik looks triumphantly at me: So, did you get a pay increase?

He has, this year again, he tells me and says at the same time that he's going to shell out for new alloys

124

when the next pay comes through, he's already checked some out. He's exalted, all pumped up.

He doesn't come here as often any more, but I know that he still calls it home, even if he now has another one too. But he's still peeled this place off himself quicker than I would have thought. The fact alone that he was going to start studying was surprising. When I think about it now, he fits better in the category of those who live here. Stay here. Don't leave.

The summer evenings are of course endless here. On the horizon of the lake there are several boats bobbing along. The fishing is something else at night, I'm told. One of the boats gets closer to the jetty in the bay where I'm sitting on a rock. It has been an unusually warm day and the heat is still hanging in the air. I'm listening to music and haven't spoken to anyone for several hours and don't want to do so now either, so I get up and go before the boat docks. I walk the short distance back to the village, but there is nowhere to hide here, nowhere to keep out of the way if you don't want to speak to anyone, so I go home and pull down the floral blind and try to become tired.

43

There is something special about staying here. Failure is the wrong word, but many of those who have remained here have a ready-prepared defence speech. The longer I stay here, the closer I get to mine.

There are so many different realities. My life now which has nothing to do with my previous life. What I experience here, which almost no one back home can understand. But nobody here either. He who once knew everything but now knows nothing. That which is outwardly visible which maybe some people, a few, manage to notice when I move amongst them. But that which is my life is isolated from everything else.

No one knows, no one wonders, no one asks.

There are plenty of superficial questions and I am starting to be good at superficial answers.

And silence can always be filled. There is TV, there are cars, the Hotel, the shop. Music.

It isn't uncommon that I leave the CD player on at the same time as the TV. One of them a bit louder, as if there is a thought behind it, as if I was listening to that one. But it's not always the case. The important thing is that there is noise, something which drowns out the fridge's insistent humming every half hour, something which takes away unasked questions and empty answers.

That's why the nights awake are also so wide awake. Silent, acute, harsh. Relentless.

People here like cloudberries. Cloudberries with vanilla ice cream is the best dessert, but I'm not fond of the "forest's gold", hard as I try.

When Lena invites me round for dinner once again, there are cloudberries for dessert. *Kaffeost* and cloudberries, but Lena puts a pastry from the shop on a plate in front of me. It can take a bit of time, she says, to learn everything.

Christmas comes so suddenly, or maybe it feels late because it has been winter for so long here when December arrives. I'm leaving here and have taken a week off. Christmas Eve is on a Tuesday and on the Sunday I start the journey that will last until Monday. The bus to the coast is full of people and paper bags full of Christmas presents.

I come across my driving license photos, the card with four pictures, one cut out, and I don't remember that they were in colour. It's a year later and I see the picture occasionally on my license, but in black and white and it's not often I have to show ID, never here.

The colour photos are detached from what I see in the mirror.

There in the walk-in freezer it's as if I can't get enough air. As if my breathing isn't sufficient. I stop what I'm doing, let the Alaskan Pollock fall back down into the brown box and try to focus on breathing. Deep breaths in, deep out. In through the nose, out through the mouth. But the air isn't enough. I wrestle off the fleece top and gloves, forget that the door handle is cold, remember that when I open the door and my fingers nearly stick. Try again outside the freezer. Deep breaths. But it doesn't help. Not at first, but sometimes it does help, because after I've swapped jobs with Stina, who has just arrived and prefers working in the storeroom like this after the weekend, when I've started unpacking her cart by the preserves shelves, suddenly I remember. And feel at the same time that my breaths are enough now, I'm getting enough air. And I don't remember when it became ok again.

44

Two days before my birthday, I remember it and think that I'm the only one who will. The only one here. When the day comes, I get several calls and messages from home, my old from home, and at work Sonia actually says happy birthday. She does it in the break room on the first break and at first I don't understand what she is saying. She smiles to me: I do write the pay checks and have seen your social security number quite a few times.

She points to the table and a foil platter with freshly baked pastries.

After work I buy sweets from Olle's, more than I need. I take a long shower, Mona isn't home, and then I climb into bed with my bag of sweets and an episode of Murder Mysteries which I've definitely already seen, but which are still totally ok.

When I wake up it's one o'clock and I can't be bothered getting up to brush my teeth. Just when I'm starting to fall back to sleep my mobile beeps. Belated happy returns. From one of the few numbers I know by heart, which is there unused under his name.

The forest is an empty space. A breathing room, a break, even if it does not offer me anything like that. Yet. I guess that it will happen, that I'll end up coming across paths, that are not visible, aren't even paths, between the trees, know my way, place my feet in the right places and feel at home. Now I'm only visiting. Like an uninvited guest who nobody notices. It's quiet and calm here. Even quieter. As soon as I get sufficiently far from the road, as far as I dare to go, all sounds vanish. It's just the forest and nature left now. When I get up to the top of a peak I can see the ice, that I know is there under the snow. The mountain in the distance, covered in snow, the additional isolation which also silences me. Being here is to leave reality.

45

Already before I moved here I'd come across, here in the village, the street with the shop and the pizzeria and the other street where the chemist is. I didn't go to the surrounding areas, I never went there, hardly do now, but knew the area.

I knew it as much as I needed and need now. I'm not learning so much anymore and am not getting to know the nature at all.

It's too big, too new, too unknown. It doesn't open up to me.

Mona has knocked on my door and when I open and got to say hi I can't get a sound out. I need to clear my throat, cough, my voice is stuck somewhere inside. I've not spoken in two days. Before I manage to say anything she invites me in for a *fika*. It's the first time, I recognise the smell of fresh baking from her part of the house.

My pile of unread books on the nightstand is growing. I want to read, but I don't do it. I don't know what I do to get the time to pass but it passes. There are new days and new evenings and soon I've at least seen all the Murder Mysteries that Lena leant me. As I've been watching them, we've discussed each episode during our coffee breaks. When I get close to the last episode I don't really want to see it.

At the end of the summer Finn colours his hair black. He does it when he's at the coast, at Joachim's, one weekend. In some way it's the last sign that he's going to leave here. But he has a year left at school.

I'm not showing any signs at all.

I'm at the second hand shop and am trying to find a small storage unit for the kitchen. I don't know exactly what I'm looking for and wander aimlessly around the large store. The space is bigger than they need for the stock and so there is plenty of room.

I can hardly remember anymore what I fell for with him. What it was that made me want to be with him and by extension to leave something, almost everything, to come here and be with him.

When I think about it now I still can't figure out what my type is. What I'm looking for.

But I'm not looking either, maybe that's it, maybe that's why I don't know what I'm looking for. I don't feel any need for it and it doesn't happen of its own accord, like it often used to. I wasn't looking for him either.

I run my hand over different pieces of furniture but don't fancy any of them. Before I go out to the car, I do buy a ceramic bowl that looks like it's from the

50s. Mainly so that the woman who works here, whose name I actually don't know, has something to do.

Laila has a shrill voice that means she's normally the one who gets heard. In the break room she always takes over even though I don't think she means to. It's partly her voice but also her way of trying to get everyone involved in the conversation.

No one tries to encroach on her style. Some are busy with other conversations but answer when she says 'right?' with a challenging voice. Even though I've worked here for more than a year, I don't always end up part of her inquisitions.

Marie is reading a gossip magazine and is leafing carefully through it with the tip of her long, painted nails so that the magazine can still be sold afterwards. Laila has already asked if everyone doesn't agree that the price of milk has actually gone up a bit too much over the last year, but now she wants everyone to agree with her that it goes without saying who's behind the latest wave of break-ins in the county. Diplomatic, mumbled nos when she looks out across the table. With questions like this she wouldn't ever look my way. I want to contradict her but can't. Instead I bite harder into my pear and look out of the window.

It's strange to think that regardless of how your life looks, there are certain things that you have to do. When I'm sitting clipping my toenails one free Sunday, I start thinking about the stuffed bear. In some way I just can't quite forget about it.

135

I also need to cook, or at least get round to eating something. When I eat lunch at home it's almost always instant noodles. At work I try to vary my meals mainly for the sake of my colleagues. Or their impression of me. My dinners don't have a name, or a recipe. Sometimes it's a stew, sometimes a sauce, but there's always garlic and ginger in the dinners. I don't get fed up of it, but it doesn't really taste of much either.

I gather up the nail clippings in a pile on the lino floor and when I throw them away I see the bear's claws in front of me.

46

Sitting at the till can sometimes be a meditative experience. Not that I've spent time meditating, but it's how I imagine it. How the world disappears and your thoughts are blurred out. I pass the shopping, one item at a time, in front of the barcode reader. Weigh the fruit and vegetables. And the bags of sweets. Say hi and thanks and it'll be so much and here's your change. Smile and look the customers in the eye. But am not there. But nowhere else either.

In the fridge too, wearing the warming fleece in the same blue colour as our vests, the monotonous work becomes a form of meditation. Pushing the dairy products forward so that they come to the front of the shelves, those with the earliest date furthest forward. I don't meet anyone here either, but between the milk, yoghurt and cream, I can of course recognise and study the customers without them, usually, noticing me. And it's from here that I see Emelie one Friday. He has come home, without letting me know and she holds him by the arm, they are happy, but I can see his eyes, that he's looking for me and does not want to look too happy if I spot him. She looks nice and it seems like a good thing, it doesn't bother me that they are here. And I'd like to tell him, that he doesn't need to hold his happiness in, that he doesn't need to be worried about me, but I know that it would sound like I mean the opposite. Even to him, who is still the one who knows me the best. Maybe he doesn't know me that well.

I can't sleep. We've been to the Hotel and I should be tired, but I'm nothing, not wide-awake, not tired. After a moment or several hours in bed, I get up and go to the bathroom. I don't really need the toilet but I can't keep just lying there.

I sit on the toilet seat with the lid down. The floor feels so close and suddenly that's where I am. I don't fall, but land. It's cold against my bare legs, against my arms. I don't know how long I lie there, but after a while I hear Mona coming down the stairs. I flush the toilet and dash out before Mona gets down the stairs. Crawl under the duvet and into bed.

When I wake up it's eleven o'clock and I have bruises on my knees.

Sometimes I forget to turn off the TV when I go to work, I often sleep with it turned on. I never forget to turn it on, because the silence is so present.

Frost is eating at the window when I wake up and I've dreamt of another time which is not now. I had never moved here and it's as if I had to have this dream to realise that I chose to move here. That it was my will that brought me here and not chance.

That I met him was chance, but that we did something with that chance was a choice. That we believed in it was love but that it ended was not fatigue. Not boredom.

It's cold on the floor and I'm wearing woollen socks which his mother gave me. My dressing gown is made of fleece and is warming too. Like every morning, I have buttered toast and tea. The TV is on but I don't see it, I'm looking out the window where in one corner I can see part of the street outside. The odd car drives by and even fewer people walk past.

When they have stopped asking me why I moved here, it happens occasionally that I'm asked about him. Because of course they know him. Here I can say 'they' without specifying who 'they' are, because everyone who at some point asks me these things knows him. They know him and not me, even though I now have some of their numbers in my phone. Even though I've been invited over to Stina's and even though I ride in Kalle's car to the Hotel on Saturdays. It's him they know, and when he is home it's him they speak to.

They sometimes ask why it ended, how it feels for me now. Stina does so one time at the Hotel. Lars isn't there that Saturday and we've gone down into the bear room. First she calls Lars, who is at the coast and sounds drunk, then they get onto the way she talks to him and their conversation goes nowhere. Stina hangs up and turns to me and I stop looking at the bear and stir the straw round my glass.

She wonders if I shouldn't forget about him

now and try to find someone else and I smile because I'm surprised because I've never thought about that. And I say to her that I have forgotten about him and that I really don't need to sit here on a Saturday night talking about him.

The bear looks resigned from this angle.

Finn and I empty the bottle recycling machine. I think that it's the last time we'll do this together; he finishes up next week.

Maybe I've stopped enjoying detective shows. Or else it's just because I've seen all the VHS tapes at least once that I've stopped watching them. I haven't got hold of anything new. When the TV is always on now, instead the various programs tell me what time and day of the week it is. So it's Wednesday now. But I of course know that because I've been at work and have looked at the schedule. I've just come home and winter is starting to get closer. It's dark and comforting out.

Before Christmas and before I manage to leave, he comes home. He calls me when he has been home for two days. He says that he has seen me, that he didn't think that I was still here and I tell him I'm leaving the next day. We go out in his car. He drives even though I can now too, but it's his car and he's the one who knows where you drive when you're not going anywhere.

We don't say that much. He tells me a bit about university and he asks about my life. My life.

A few hours later we stop outside my place and

when I have got out of the car and am about to shut the door, he leans over to my side and says: You know that you say *jo* instead of *ja* for 'yes' now, right?

47

I'd like to remember my emotions. Like how something hurts the body, like how it feels to be pleasantly surprised, like the intense fatigue after something fun happens. But I don't remember, I don't feel.

When I cook, I cook a lot of food. A stew that'll last the whole week or pasta sauce which I'll eat with pasta the first day, rice the second day and later maybe just the sauce on its own.

I usually eat dinner in bed, put a pillow behind my back and a pillow on my lap and the plate on top of that. With the TV on. Sometimes watch something. Fork or spoon; different consistencies, the same taste. But I eat. I eat at least.

There are so many smells in the shop which I've never known anywhere else. The smell of the rain-wet boxes in the loading bay, the smell of empty bottles and cans for recycling, stale beer and soda, a hint of yeast. The smell of meat fat which is amplified by the warm water you use to clean the meat mincer. How intensely the smell of cheap perfume lingers on a stone floor for days after a bottle has shattered. The overwhelming smell of plastic when you're unpacking new deliveries. The smell in the walk-in freezer, an indication of what food is in there, hidden in the plastic and ice. The dry, sweet smell of tobacco when you go to fetch multiple packets of blue Petterøe's in the fridge.

It's the coldest part of winter now and some days you stay indoors. You can't wash your face on those mornings and have to wear all the clothes you have if you need to leave the house. Through the window I can tell that it's one of those days. The people are scrunched up and packed in, the cars move hesitantly forwards. The thermometer shows minus thirty-seven.

I know that my bike lock won't open when it's this cold. I know that I won't be going anywhere anyway, don't need an explanation. Days like this it's nice not to have a direction, not to have a goal. I don't get dressed and let everything I do take time. I do a whole week's washing up and then watch several episodes of series that are only on during the day and which I don't follow.

In the evening I take a long shower and hold the shower head against my chest and stomach until the skin turns red. I get warmed up right into my bones. It feels like I spend too much time in the bathroom, but Mona has said repeatedly that I can take as long as I need.

48

Saturday night at the Hotel. Another one. Things are happening around me: Hi, can I buy you a drink?

A blurred gaze, I look away. Can't be bothered interacting this evening. Not more than I had to to get here. Change places, from the bar to some armchairs further away, see Stina wrapped around Lars from a distance. Who she used to talk about in the storeroom and in the car on the way here. Probably other places too, but I don't know.

The armchair's fake leather sticks to my bare arms, it's warm but the shiny material is also sticky from too many drinks. It's a night out like all the others, but now the snow is starting to melt, it's possible to walk home at night, because the cold isn't quite as intense.

When I lie awake at night I usually feel clearheaded, sharp. Still try to sleep and try to not become desperate.

A bruising pain throughout my body. I lie as still as I can, think that I'll fall asleep more easily that way.

A lot happens in the periphery. Laila complains about

the levels of taxation, Stina talks about Lars or about something car-related with Fredrik. Finn is also outside of that which counts as my life. His runs parallel to mine, and we happen to work at the same place. I don't know so much about anyone's life here. And I'm even hanging out with some of them now. I meet Stina quite often and after a while I start to spend time with Finn too. Mainly I give him lifts home so his mum doesn't have to drive in to the village and pick him up, or hang around after she's finished work and wait for him. We don't say so much in the car and he's still in the fringe too. The one that is still there.

The sun is back after its winter migration. The dark days took over for several months, and I miss out on the daylight hours when I'm working. You get used to it, but the sun's return is still just as fascinating every year. The darkness is a comfort to me. A warm embrace. I like the sun, but don't need it.

When I'm cleaning I find copies of my application letter to the shop. It feels as if I'm reading something someone else has written. Happy, creative and full of initiative. Quick learner. Most of it is probably valid, even now.

49

In a way, is a relief that I'm not invited to what I guess is Finn's leaving party. Given that I don't think Stina is invited, I'd have to go there alone if I wanted to go.

There's another whodunit on the TV and floral blind is pulled down.

Sometimes everything feels like it's on standby. I go here, I live here, live here waiting for something. But I have no idea of what that something is. It becomes especially clear when I count down the weekdays, like a sort of holding pattern before the next week. But I'm not waiting on anything in particular. No day where something will happen, no changes on the horizon.

50

The nights have become much darker, the light at midnight is just a memory, but the absence of light can keep me awake too. I close my eyes. Listen to the silence. The odd car in the distance, the fridge humming on and off. Sometimes I forget and am surprised at how little time has passed. Or how much. Sometimes I must have fallen asleep.

Then a car gets closer. Not an engine sound I recognise, but the car stops near Mona's house. The motor idling. I look at the clock, it's half past midnight. I haven't slept. I sit up in bed, the car is still there and I hear someone go out and slam the door shut. Then a shout and then an answer from someone else. After a while the car doors shutting again and then the screeching against asphalt as the car drives off.

All autumn I get nosebleeds in the morning. Putting a wad of paper in my left nostril when I sit up in the morning becomes a habit, there is a roll of toilet paper next to the bed. When I have to go to the store, I throw the paper in the toilet.

51

The air doesn't feel fusty, it's only when I unlock the main door and go out that the air there is so fresh. I've been off for three days and sick for one and haven't been out. I think about spring, a rebirth, the one that never comes here. Don't know if it means anything, maybe more that it isn't that, spring is not a regeneration, anywhere. I miss it, but here too nature survives during all seasons. Without spring flowers here, of course.

No crocuses or anemones. No buttercups or coltsfoot.

But the grass is green in the summer.

And the fresh air here is fresh thanks to the snow. And the ice. I think. I cross the street and see Stina on the pallets with a cigarette in her hand and the communal smokers' jacket over her shoulders. She nods hello and I tap in the code which opens the door. The new stock has just arrived and Sonia asks me to take the freezer. The fleece top, the gloves, the cart with the stock. The air is cold and still, like it has always been in here, it's never swapped out. I take the worn Stanley knife out of the fleece pocket and open the first box.

52

They're renovating the hotel, so it's closed for a week. The décor is being changed, the drab and tired décor. It's going to be a fresh design that is in line with the Hotel's profile, it says in the paper. The Hotel's manager does not believe that the old interior suited the modern individual. There is a photo where the manager is standing next to one of the old armchairs, in his hand he has a picture of a white leather pouffe. The bear looms behind him.

Several weeks have passed since Finn finished at work, so he could move to London. There's not much of a difference at the shop, other than that no one has black hair anymore. A new part timer has arrived, from the same town as Finn. They're cousins and you can tell, but they're not otherwise very alike. He's called Stefan and he talks a lot. He mainly talks to Fredrik, mainly about cars. He's had his license for several months but has always driven.

It's rare that I need anything. I buy food in the shop and sweets at Olle's on Saturdays and other than that I don't often need anything. I manage with what I have even if I forget to buy food. There's always something I can eat, I'm not fussy. So I've only been a few times to either of the two gas stations. I've mainly been there for petrol and haven't gone in.

One of the petrol stations is open until nine and the other until ten and after that everything is closed, apart from the Hotel of course. One evening I have such a craving for yoghurt that I decide to visit the one with the later opening. It's not far to either of them, a bit more so to the one I'm going to, I have to cross the main road, the one that goes to the coast or to Norway and I do so at a spot without a footbridge to save a few metres. It's dark out and the snow hasn't arrived yet, just the streetlamps light the way. There are never many cars out and I think that I've looked both ways properly but when I'm walking over, at a fair pace, a car comes from the direction of the coast and has to swerve a bit over into the other lane and the driver honks their horn. It's a metallic blue car, the alloys display an interest in cars, as does the sound, that much I've learned about cars in my time here.

At the gas station there's just one kind of yoghurt, strawberry flavour. I buy the local paper and a bar of chocolate and walk home again. Look more carefully and run over the road.

53

Usually I manage to keep my thoughts at bay. I can't handle getting into where they can lead. Feeling that I'm in the wrong place. Feeling that I should do something. Just something. Small. Change. But the TV's babbling and the darkness usually do as a distraction.

Cleaning the meat mincer is the worst job at the shop. It's tough as the mincer and all its parts weigh a fair bit and it's a fiddly job to get it all clean. So you take your time over the job. An hour before closing time I sometimes say that I can do it. Most of the others don't like the job, so it's appreciated that I do it voluntarily.

The bits of meat lose their colour in the warm water, get washed down the drain. No other noise beside the water running into the stainless steel sink.

When I've slept badly every night for a week, I give up going to bed. It's Friday and I'm working on Saturday but I can't bring myself to lie awake staring at the ceiling for another night. I've got no plan for what I'll do.

First I watch almost a whole film, but then I turn it off and put a CD on instead. I'm tired but don't let it fool me, I need to get more tired before I can try and sleep. I dig around at the back of the wardrobe and find a blue nail varnish, almost the same colour as the vests at work. When I've painted my finger nails I take my socks off and paint my toe nails too. When I look at the alarm clock it's four and the next second it goes off. I'm clothed when I wake up and the nail varnish has marks from the folds in the sheets. I've slept three hours.

Fredrik has five CDs in his car and they're all called something to do with dance or trance and all have the same aesthetic. He's asked me to choose some music and I finally go for Dance Revolution. The stereo spits out a disc that's the same style and I can't hear any difference in the music. Even though I haven't been to the coast so many times, I recognise the route. How the trees stand, the long haired barley at one spot, signs showing the way to places I've never seen. Place names which sound like nothing like the place names where I used to live.

Two days earlier Fredrik mentioned that he was going to the coast for the weekend, to see a friend who had moved there and I'd asked if I could go along. Said that I can pay for petrol, but he just waved that away.

My almost empty rucksack at my feet. He's staying overnight, but I'm taking the bus home the same evening. Don't know what I'll do, but feel satisfied that I'm doing something.

People don't ring the doorbell here, you come over and

go in, or possibly knock and call out a hello inside the doorway. Maybe stop with the car outside, the motor running. I know that because that's how it worked in the past, when I was here to see him, when I got to know the place, or at least got an introduction.

My door is quiet and untouched and locked.

After a year has passed, I'm still living in Mona's house. I have stopped looking through the adverts in the local paper. I feel comfortable, in the sense that it feels like home. Nothing has visibly changed, the same furniture and the same blinds. I don't think about him so much, but occasionally he comes to the village and usually we'll see one another. In a way it's out of a sense of duty, mainly on his side. He never says so, but I understand that he still feels responsible, that I ended up here, that I stayed here and that he left. That I stayed here alone. That he is paying off some sort of debt by meeting me when he comes here. I could of course stop meeting him, come up with an excuse when he asks if we should see each other, but I'm not ready for that.

Meeting him still does something for me.

54

The coast is windy and noisy as usual, unknown people, anonymity. Fredrik has dropped me off in the town centre and I walk aimlessly round the streets.

During the coldest part of my second winter I rarely leave home when I'm not working. It's not the cold that keeps me in, I have clothes which should cover me down to minus twenty-five if I'm moving, but it's easier to not go out.

Time passes, even when it does so slowly. The dark and the narrow strips of light on the ceiling, a constant; if a car drives past, a change. Otherwise the never-ending time and the never-ending silence. All my sounds so clear, the sheets which rustle if I move, my breathing. The sound a reminder of the silence. But I never turn to my left, that's where the alarm clock is and I try to not look at the clock when I wake up at night. Keep looking at the light strips on the ceiling. Try to think away the silence and fail each time.

The postcard is completely black apart from the text,

"London by night," in white in one corner. Finn hasn't written that much, that he's arrived, that it's going well, that he hopes he isn't missed too much at work.

But he's sent the card to my house.

It's Thursday and we've been unpacking stock all morning. I stuff the boxes into the press and make them into a manageable load. Lena comes out from the deli with a trolley full of boxes: How's it going, have you finished watching all the Murder Mysteries?

And I admit that I have. It feels like an admission as I know that it's an acknowledgement that we no longer have this in common. In a way, I'm afraid that we'll no longer talk during *fika* breaks, that there will be silence as soon as I've finished with all the episodes.

She smiles to me: I've taped a new series; I think you'll like it.

55

At the shop, nothing is ever finished. As soon as I've organised the shelves in one aisle, I can start on the next; as soon as all the frozen goods are filled up, there are spaces to be filled in the dairy shelves. Sometimes it's frustrating that nothing is ever complete, but usually it feels comforting. That there is always something to do. That there is always something I can do.

There is no time to just wander round the shop, no time to just sit down. There is always a goal.

For a change, I take a bath after work. Mona is out when I come home, I don't actually know that much about her but she has said that she's involved in a missionary charity which knits socks. On Tuesday evenings she's always out for several hours, which is why I dare to take a bath without feeling like I'll be in the way.

The warm water wraps itself around me in an unexpected fashion when I climb into the pink bathtub. It must be years since I last took a bath. When I think harder about it, I can't remember the last time it happened. I try to feel out what I think about it, what I used to think about taking a bath, but I don't feel anything, remember anything. It's a bit too hot in the water, I get goosebumps and I can feel that I'm tensing up. Stretch my legs and try to relax. Close my eyes and wake up with my teeth chattering. I hear Mona knocking something together in her kitchen. Get up and let the water run down the drain.

What I don't have here is the background hum. Constant, grinding; sounds which pick up where the previous one ended, for ever. The sound of a city, which is witness to movement, life and everything but motion-lessness. The hum you don't even hear.

Here the silence takes over, creeps in every-where, doesn't leave me alone.

The silence which is broken by engine sounds and bass sounds from a newly installed subwoofer. But always with the silence which eventually creeps through again.

Spending so much time alone should mean that I learn everything about myself. But it's the opposite. Because day in, day out I go through the same situations, I react in the same way. I don't learn anything new.

56

I had never looked at this part of the map when I met him. Now I am here on the map. In the small dot that shows places that aren't cities. The little dot which fits me, and all the others who I know by name but no more, and my life, the main part of my life which contains some, or mostly, things that I struggle to put into words. And so much else. It's right here.

After having woken and lain awake several nights in a row, I almost get used to it. Don't feel especially tired in the morning and am surprised when one day I wake up and it's seven o'clock. I've slept the whole night.

It's more than two weeks since I last slept a whole night through and it feels empty. I'm not more alert than usual and it's almost like I've missed something. As if the time I'm awake at night is necessary, has some meaning. I stick a ball of paper in my left nostril and get up for a bowl of *filmjölk*.

I stack the shelves. Pull the stock forward to the edge so it looks full on the shelf. It's Sunday, Stina and I are working and it's dead. I'm the only one out in the shop as Stina is half drunk from last night, or maybe just drunk and is sitting in the stockroom. I told her to, because she smells of alcohol and it's best she doesn't speak to customers.

We were of course at the Hotel on Saturday because we always are, but I'm just tired whereas Stina is still stuck in Saturday night.

The autumn is a parenthesis. Waiting for winter, for the snow. Autumn is never long here, but just before it lets winter in is when it's darkest. The snow makes the sky lilac, without it it's so black. Several days feel like the end of autumn, that's what people in the shop say, now the snow is coming. It's dark when I get home, I boil mushroom stock in a pan that's too big, the other one's dirty, and add a portion of noodles. I eat in bed and flick through a magazine. When I've finished eating and drunk a glass of water, I get stomach ache. At first it sneaks up on me, but it quickly becomes more intense and soon I can no longer sit up. I lie down and try to breathe steadily, and after a while it feels a bit better. It takes a long time for me to realise that I've forgotten to put the TV on. The remote control is on the nightstand and when I hear the familiar but unknown voices, my stomach pains almost completely cease. I stare up at the ceiling and let go of the remote control. The lamp in the kitchen area and the TV are the only lights. I close my eyes.

It's as if my reality mainly feels unreal. This village which I hard barely heard of a few years ago which is now the place where I live. This silence which envelops me, which I didn't know existed. I cycle along the road and try to remember how he used to drive. Where he used to park the car. I think I've found the spot and go into the forest; mosquitoes follow me. Here you can see water almost wherever you are and the land is hilly. I walk up and down hills and pick up a stick which I drag through the earth behind me.

But I don't know anything about the place. I don't have it in me, in my blood. When I was with him, it was as if I could feel it, through him felt that I was a part of something, but without him I don't belong here.

It's damp in the grass but the air is warm and the forest is not mine, even if I thrive here. I turn back towards my bike with the lunch pack unopened in my rucksack.

57

I have low blood pressure, the doctor tells me and asks what it is usually. But I don't know, can't remember when I would last have checked or when I would have been at the doctor's or a hospital. And then I tell her about the thing with my breathing. That it's sometimes hard to catch my breath. And she listens to my breathing but doesn't hear anything wrong: It can also be up here, the problem.

And she points at her head.

I can tell by the footsteps that it's Fredrik who is coming into the break room: What are you thinking about?

In fact, right then I'm just thinking how maybe it's his aftershave that gives him away before his slightly sluggish gait, depending on which way the wind is blowing, but inside it's his footsteps that let on. But I say that I'm not thinking about anything, nothing in particular.

When it's at its darkest, I hardly ever see daylight. Daylight only just exists, just a few hours a day, if I'm at the till I can see out through the large glass doors, can see that it is actually light.

It takes such a long time before I change the lightbulb in the hall. I forget to buy bulbs, even though I write it on my hand. Then it sits there in its packaging on the chair inside the door for two weeks before I get on with it.

I know where everything is in the hall and pretty quickly get used to the dark. When I decide to get on with changing the bulb it's evening and the daylight has already been gone for some time. My mobile in one hand and the lightbulb in the other. I stand on the chair and eventually get the bulb in. It's a bit messier than I remember when I turn the light on.

My memories of him don't fade, they just become more and more unimportant every day. Sometimes I wonder which thoughts have taken his place, but never really come up with an answer.

58

It's noisy and raucous and I feel quieter than ever. Lars is having some sort of barbecue party in what I guess is his parents' house. THIS IS LIFE! someone without a shirt on shouts from the balcony and people turn to him and raise their beer cans and laugh. It feels like everyone is here.

I've lost Stina somewhere and have finished my beer and even though I know I could get another one from anyone, I don't know who I should ask. I get up from my spot on the grass, hear fragments of conversation as I walk up the slope, towards the house. It is a semi-underground house and I go into the basement, under the balcony. Groups of people in every room, in every space. Stina with Lars in the sauna, I hear them as I go past. One floor up it's a bit calmer, some empty rooms and suddenly a closed door with no one behind it. I go in and shut the door behind me. Lars' childhood bedroom, it must be. A narrow bed with a cover, a desk with a computer, a bookshelf with books for someone younger. Snow scooter magazines. The trace in the dust when I run my finger along the books on the shelf.

I lie down on the bed, the effect of the beer

feels more than I remember having had. I close my eyes.

I don't remember having locked the door, but I wake to the sound of knocking and rattling the door handle: What the hell? Open up!

And my mobile's display shows that several hours have passed. Outside stands Lars, Stina in the background, she's laughing in that way that she does when she's drunk. Lars mainly looks surprised now, but pulls Stina into the room with him and locks the door again.

Out on the balcony the noise has changed in tone but the sky is still just as bright and someone shouts THIS IS LIFE! again.

59

I only see the northern lights here once. It's just at the start when I moved here. It's so strong and stretches over the whole sky and shows colours I've never seen before. The others can't ever compare with this. The others aren't pale copies or imitations; they aren't even close. Sometimes I think that it might be like that first time, but I give up hoping after a few months.

Enjoy yourself, it's later than you think. Enjoy yourself, while you're still in the pink. The years go by, as quickly as you wink. The song in my headphones so upbeat. *Enjoy yourself, enjoy yourself, it's later than you think.* I start to cry.

Part three

60

Sonia and I are working this evening. She doesn't usually work after five, but Marie is sick and the summer staff haven't started yet. I'm going through the unsold newspapers and see that, from her place at the till, she looks several times at the clock above the exit. Just a few minutes left. It's almost empty in the shop. When I see her head twist towards the clock again, I ask her if she wants to go, say that I can close up myself. She gives me a big smile and says that it's not really allowed, that there's always supposed to be at least two in the shop, that she, of all people, should know that. But that it would be really great. There's a meeting with the kennel club. And she's the chairperson. And Marie isn't here and it seems quiet.

I sit at the till and see her hurry through the shop towards the stockroom, at the same time as she takes off the vest. There's only one customer left and just as I think I've seen, it's Lena's husband, who's hurrying forward in the aisles and makes it to the till at a minute past seven, apologetically: It's funny that it ends up like this when your missus works in the shop.

When he has put the last item in his plastic bag

175

and gone out through the automatic doors, I turn off the till and lock up. Go into the stockroom, count the money and do everything that has to be done before I leave my blue vest in the changing room and put my sandals on.

It's warm when the stockroom door opens. I lock up and leave the loading bay. The sun won't go down for several hours.

It's Friday evening and I do a full load of laundry. The sound of the washing machine is calming and comforting. The rhythmic, muffled sound. It will take more than an hour but I like it down here and don't need to go up whilst it's running. It's cool and dark, I leave the light switch untouched. I sit on a rolled up rug which is lying next to the wall on the cold concrete floor.

61

I think there have been four or five Saturdays without the Hotel when I suddenly want to go again. It's hard to put my finger on what it is that draws me in. It's not to avoid comments and suggestions, it's not the punch-up that will probably happen before closing time.

I consider for a while what will attract the least attention, going there on my own or that I get in touch with Stina. I have no explanation for why I wouldn't want to go myself, no valid explanation and I should have one.

Finally, I call. Stina sounds a bit surprised, but doesn't ask more, just says that they'll come and a few hours later I hear Kalle's car.

62

It's not like me, but at the same time neither do I know what is like me. What I am, beside my routines. I know that he has been drinking, I know that everyone at the Hotel has been drinking, that's why you're here, but I still accept a lift. Stina has left the Hotel, when and with whom I don't know, but she's my ticket to Kalle's car, Kalle who actually never seems to drink when he drives, and now I don't have any way of getting home. Or at least back down to the village. Walking home in the dark isn't tempting.

I certainly must have looked lost at the cloakroom. Phone in one hand, trying to think if I knew the number for the taxi. He comes over to me. I know who he is of course, there's hardly anyone who I don't know by name now. He knows Kalle and we have been at a party at Stina's together and he's often at the Hotel, but we have not spoken. He's called Tim and I know that he usually drives home drunk.

And I say that I'd like to ride with him down to the village. In spite of the beer glass in his hand and in spite of the fact that his breath smells of spirits when he stands a bit too close and asks me.

The windows' latches make me think of something, the feeling when you close and open them. I have three windows in my home and it has taken until now for me to realise that I should clean them. Because when I think about it, they probably needed cleaning already when I moved in.

Mona isn't the type to stand on a chair with a bucket of water and a cloth. She's determined, but her leg isn't up to it, she has a stick in one hand when she takes the stairs; if it's sat at the bottom of the stairs I know that she's on that floor, if it's not then I know she's upstairs.

It's my second missed spring. The air is cold and I'm wearing lots of clothes, I get sweaty from getting up onto and down from the chair, but I'm cold when I stand still for too long.

When I have dinner that evening, in bed, the streetlights are extra bright through the window.

There is a duality in the pride that many people here feel for the place. Maybe like the feelings for a sibling. You can talk crap about the place, but if someone from outside says something bad, the pride comes out. Then it is important to be from here.

63

The signs of sorrow on Stina after the funeral are not
that visible. Maybe there is grief there, but she doesn't
show any of the usual signs. She doesn't work any slower
and she doesn't get stuck going through the motions.
But on the next occasions that I see her drinking, at the
Hotel, she drinks more quickly than usual, more than
usual and more spirits. And there's something in her
look. Maybe it's always there but it's at the Hotel that I
see it. There is something dark, something like how they
usually describe there being hate in someone's eyes.

The TV is on as usual but I don't take in whatever is
on. I realise this when I suddenly hear what someone
says; it's nothing particular, but I react to the fact that
I am reacting.

Once I knew everything about someone other than
myself, but I don't anymore. During the time that has
passed since we broke up, a lot has of course happened
in his life. Of which I know, am aware of, only a
fraction. Slivers here and there, some he has talked
about, others which I've heard about, certain things

I've guessed my way to.

The few things I do know don't mean much to me, because I know that for every day that passes, loads of things are happening in his life about which I know nothing. Which mean that the whole time I know less and less about him. A thought which sometimes is frustrating, but mainly satisfying, given I no longer care.

I try to remember if they sell clothes at the second hand shop. There are two plastic bags of clothes which I have cleared out. Totally fine clothes, but which I haven't worn in a long time. If even at all since I came here. I put the bags on the back seat and reverse out of Mona's driveway. It's hot in the car and I wind down the window, it's a bit stiff, almost sticks, but gives way and the cooler air floods in.

It's easy to breathe. The air feels almost as clear and sharp as a cloudless winter's day, even though it's summer. I'm alone on the road towards the industrial park. The road grey, the asphalt potholed here and there. But straight. Simple.

The Hotel isn't as important in the summer, even if it is open. The light nights are made for house parties and barbecues. Occasionally I get invited, off the cuff, but I have an inner barrier which makes it difficult for me to go. It's normally via Stina that I am invited, in the lunchroom over a microwave meal, when the subject of the weekend comes up.

But I'm never the one directly invited and in people's houses there is no bear room to go to.

182

My evenings are my walks. On Saturdays too.

One Saturday evening when I'm out for a walk, I feel the urge to walk towards the Hotel. I look at my clothes, I've left the jogging bottoms at home, my jeans look clean and the top is ok. It's the first time I walk up the hill. And the first time I go to the Hotel on my own. The road curls round the mountain and as it's summer and light, I dare to take a shortcut through the woods. Halfway up I think about turning back. Not just because I've become more out of breath than I'd expected, but I don't know who is at the Hotel either.

The reindeer ceased seeming strange quite quickly. On the way to the neighbouring town they're always standing there, in a herd, often on the road. They aren't there for the salt, the roads aren't gritted in the inlands, but they are still there.

64

Fredrik doesn't say that much during the day. The few customers who come into the shop, at the checkout I see that it's mainly necessities, no deviation, they too are reserved. It's been more than a week since the accident, but the day of the funeral refreshes everything. Crystallises, lights up. The portrait which is certainly stood on the coffin at the front of the church, the one that everyone who leaves a rose on the coffin sees. The picture of someone living, who now is not. I've only been to one funeral, one which everyone was expecting but which of course still brought out tears. This funeral no one expected. Which is why everyone's eyes are emptier today. Their looks more distant. But at the same time I know that it is not the first time that it has happened. Young men who leave the place earlier than expected.

Summer comes round again before I remember my walks. I look for an outfit that suits the weather and under several layers of clothes, I find the MP3 player on which I used to listen to music during the walks. Those put on ice. Although that's not right. The cold has never hindered me. Nothing has hindered me, really. It's just worked well, staying in.

I've been free all day and haven't planned on doing anything special in the evening, so I plug the MP3 player in to charge and eat yoghurt in front of the TV for a while. Then I go out.

65

If I see him when he's here, I react. It's May and could have been summery in another place, but here the ice is breaking up and the snow is melting at the moment. I see him driving a car that I haven't seen earlier, guess it must be his new one. And I feel something. I try to put that feeling into words, I know that I'm over him, but at the same time he's the only one here, even if he's hardly here anymore, with whom I have any such relation. Someone that I know so much about because he told me it all himself and because I experienced it. No second hand sources. We knew everything about each other.

The feeling doesn't hurt, it's not longing either, at least not for him. We are done. We were done with each other a long time ago and if we had just admitted it to ourselves a little earlier, I would never have lived here.

He drives past me on the road from the village to the school, I'm out for a stroll. He beeps and waves.

One day I see a child, or a teenager, take some bars of chocolate and put them inside his jacket. I'm just coming around the corner to the shelves of sweets, the part you can't see from the till and I try to recall whether we have a procedure for how I should handle this. But I can't remember and instead go automatically over to him and grab his arm. He jumps. I recognise him, but here recognising someone means less than not doing so. He looks hopelessly at me and I take him into the storeroom without saying anything. It's the afternoon and empty in the shop. I make him wait in the small room, where we count up the till, while I fetch Sonia. She only needs to see him from behind: Oh you, that wasn't much of a surprise.

But she sounds quite kind when she says it.

Before the ice gives up for the year, my second non-spring, some of the last weeks when people drive on it, I walk out on the ice. It's almost midnight and I actually have slept but woke up, as usual, and decided to go out. Ski trousers and winter coat over my pyjamas, hat, the two scarves, gloves and winter boots. It's not completely dark out, the street light spreads its amber rays further than the lights would appear to be able to in the dark, and in one of my gloves my phone, like a weak torch with no direction. The sky is lilac.

It's absolutely silent, except for the sound of my steps in the snow on the ice. I walk where it's neither been ploughed or sprayed up by cars, just next to me is the ice road. I don't go far out, stay close to the land which I know is underneath, know because I'm familiar with this place now. It's difficult for me to let go of the fear completely, it is not a natural position for me to be out on the ice, but the fear is not as cramp-like as my white knuckles the first few times I went along in a car out on the ice, a skidding car.

And there is another feeling besides the fear as well.

What surprised me most afterwards, is how long it has been since someone touched me. There is not really anything loving in what happened, but the feeling was so novel that it lingers for several days. I think that maybe it will happen again and that maybe it will happen with Tim again. But two weeks later he is gone.

66

When it happens here, when the wrong person dies, someone who is too young, it happens everywhere. Across the whole village and almost out in the surrounding nature. The pines seem wearier and the lakes deeper. Distances increase and decrease. I walk alone in the nature that it so close to the village that I left the car at home and walked here. I am not involved in this grief. I should really only know that Tim was one of Kalle's best friends, how he looked and that he used to get into fights at the Hotel on Saturdays. That he was one of those who got into fights. And actually I don't know that much else.

There is another sound in the shop now, as if all sounds are filtered, as if a lid had been placed over it. Several weeks have passed, also since the funeral, but it's clear that it will stay like this for a while yet. Even if nobody says anything. Even if nobody talks about it.

After the renovations, the Hotel is more like something from my old home town. More city. The walls which were previously wood panelled are now painted white. Wallpaper with a silver pattern and black details, and

191

white leather pouffes instead of the old faux leather armchairs. The bar stainless steel and cold.

There's an offer on a new cocktail for the opening. Everyone who does not have a beer in their hand is drinking that cocktail and, other than that, not much has changed. Maybe people stand a little further from the bar. Stina Jenny Kalle have disappeared into the throng, swallowed by the mass formed by the Hotel's clientele. A sloppy, slightly messy throng, but most of all a community.

I find my way down to the basement. The renovation has ploughed ahead here too, as I can see when I come into the bear room. High tables with white, black and silver bar stools are scattered around the room. But no bear. Instead a slightly raised stage where I know there will be a DJ as soon as market Saturday comes round. I turn towards the door.

On the way back out I take the opportunity to visit the bathroom in the basement. It was Stina who showed me, of course, the toilets that are really for the staff and are only open to the Hotels guests during the market. They are around a corner at the end of a corridor and when I come round the corner I catch the eye of someone taller than myself. The strip light isn't turned on here and the light is dim and I get scared. After a few deep breaths, I dare to look up at the bear again.

Nothing in me argues when I think that I should go out. That I should do something. Maybe go for a stroll or a bike ride or maybe take the car out for a spin.

No resistance and I go out and it's warm and I can feel that the day has been warm, even if I was hardly aware of it because I've been in the shop and have mainly been dealing with frozen goods and barely looked out the window.

But there is a warmth in the asphalt.

When the truck comes in the morning I'm quick to take the large cart with soda and beer. It feels good lifting something heavy, to really use your muscles. And I know that it bothers Laila that I do it. Fredrik hardly cares.

67

It isn't dark when I finish work. I have a few hours off from having done the stock check at New Year and take them because Sonia asked me to. It isn't dark, but it's far from light. The street lights are needed, even in the middle of the day. The days I have off during the week I generally stay in. At least at this time of year. When I finish work I go straight home. So it feels strange that I'm out in the village on a day in the middle of the week in the middle of the day. I decide to not go home, challenging myself with my decision. I walk towards the schools and the library. The schoolyard is full of children. Snowballs but also footballs. It's quiet at the library. Quieter than at any library I have ever visited. A paper rustles in a corner, otherwise just the muffled keyboard taps from a computer somewhere and quiet steps at the other end of the small room which forms the library. I've never been here before.

We get a discount on food at the store. Not that much, but it's still something. Fredrik always does his food shopping on Mondays. Always the same things. Ten cans of tuna, a large pack of crisp bread, seven bananas, frozen chickens, normally three of them, six litres of milk, two one and a half litre bottles of diet soda, tomatoes and cucumbers. Never anything else in terms of food.

But on the day of the funeral I see him take a few pieces of pick and mix straight from the stand.

The few times I've been sick it's been with a fever and stuff like the flu and colds and I don't know if I can call this an illness but something is wrong. It hits hard, properly, like a punch in the stomach. I'm at work and sitting at the till and trying to remember the code for lemons when I feel that I need to lie down. Fredrik is sitting at the other till, the time is around four in the afternoon and people are on their way home from work and stop in at the shop and we need to have two tills open. I say to him that I don't feel well, that he needs to call for someone else and Stina comes quickly. When I get up I almost collapse. In the stockroom Sonia tells me to go to the clinic, that I shouldn't just go home like this. And then she says that she'll drive me, even though it's close by. Everything is close by here.

The waiting room is almost empty. Directly opposite me there's an old man sitting with a rollator in front of him. There are gossip magazines on the table and I take one and start flicking through it. A man whom I assume is a nurse comes in, I recognise him from the shop: Ah yes, you, what's your name again?

And later he has clearly worked out my name, from where I don't know, although I know now. It's just how it works, that you know. When I have told him why

I'm there and he tells me to wait and that I'll be seen within a quarter of an hour and he walks down a corridor then I remember his name too.

It's one of the few sunshine hours, one of the hours of daylight and I've taken the car out. Just outside the village, but sufficiently far that I still take the car. A place out in the nature which doesn't feel as foreign as much of the rest of it. I've been here so many times now, but I still take a moment to look at the view. There are shallow hills, stretching down into the lakes. Frozen and snow-covered now, the layer of white is everywhere, with lines of footsteps which are maybe paths when the snow is gone, and with large, untouched edges. The snow is soft and, on the trees, heavy too. Thick sheets which weigh down the branches and make some of the trunks bend. Those who live here, the ones who come from here, don't take a moment like I do. They don't think about it. They can of course think that it's beautiful, but they don't act like I do.

68

Kalle has had his driving license suspended for three months and no one else wants to go without drinking, so when Stina asks if I can drive to the Hotel I say yes. I get to drive Kalle's car, it's several years newer than mine, decades probably, and I haven't driven such a new car since I was taking lessons. The hill up to the Hotel is much easier, it's more fun driving his car and for a while it almost seems like I understand why people spend so much money on cars and on doing them up. It's almost as if I understand why Kalle needed to drive so fast.

On the way to the Hotel, there's a short stretch where I get to do sixty, but otherwise the limit's forty and I'm eager to give it more throttle. But I've never driven too quickly.

The Hotel is different now that I'm sober. Everything is grimier and the people more brazen.

It's never windy when it's twenty below here. I go for a different walk, via Lena's house. She has gone to the neighbouring town and her husband and kids are away, so I've promised to take her dog for a walk after work.

I was surprised that she asked me for help and really pleased to be able to help her.

The excitable golden retriever meets me at the door; on a chair there is a lead and bags and once we're out, I let the dog take control. It leads me between houses and trees, the snow is hard and crusty, I slip occasionally, the dog turns round to see if I'm ok, if I'm following. I'm following, I've even turned off my mp3 player because it seems rude to the dog, which is still mainly quiet, apart from a muffled panting. Finally, the dog turns toward home again, first she looks at me, slightly questioningly, I smile back and it seems to be an acceptable response. When I let her into Lena's house, I say bye and the dog wags its tail.

69

Tim doesn't leave until morning and I struggle to sleep with someone else in the room. Usually it's the silence that bothers me. Now I'm not bothered, but still awake.

It's more than a year since I last heard someone else's breathing at night. The sound of someone sleeping.

The only bear I have seen is at the Hotel. The one that has now been hidden away, the one that doesn't fit in any more. And I know loads about the forest here, the nature.

But even if I stayed and lived my life here, I'd never catch up with those who belong here.

There are of course people who moved here and who, in my eyes, still seem to have always lived here. But I'll never be one of them. They moved here for the village. I ended up here.

Against the black-blue sky, the stars are clearly visible. It's cloudless, with a cold that you can almost hear. So cold that you can't feel. I walk quickly home from the petrol station where I've been to buy chocolate. Hold tight onto it with my too thin mittens. It's Saturday and it was eight thirty before I realised that I had forgotten to go to Olle's.

70

I haven't worn cross-country skis since the obligatory winter sports classes at middle school and the bindings have probably evolved since then, but the skis I've borrowed from Lena are quite old and I clip my boots in firmly. My progress isn't quick, but it still feels strange that the snow is so compliant, just lies there, doesn't open up like when I walk on it, is silent apart from a swishing sound. It's especially pleasing when I start to go a bit faster.

I head out onto the ice, over a small lake which I've driven out to in the car. It's Finn who tipped me off about this place, his mum likes it and skis here and the tracks in the snow are well defined. It's cold and I know that I will not be able to stay out for too long, the cold will reach me through all the layers. But just now it doesn't get to me.

One night I wake up in tears, I think I was crying in a dream but my eyes are full of tears and my cheeks are wet. I cry some more from the discovery but after a few hours I fall asleep. In the morning my eyelids are swollen.

71

It is the second time that I walk up the mountain, towards the Hotel. But not to the Hotel this time. It's maybe closed, or at least there's nothing special going on there. The time is six thirty and it's Saturday morning. I walk along the road, the one which winds its way round the mountain, but not in a creepy way, more like cosy. The air is humid from the night, but it's light and if you didn't live here, it would be hard to believe that it had just been night time. A car drives past on the way up, another on the way down, otherwise no hint of life. My new shoes show no signs of chafing even though I'm walking quickly.

When I've made it to the top I walk past the Hotel to the turning circle, sit down on a large stone and look out over the place. The village and its surroundings.

72

It's the first time and even though I have all the time in the world, I can't be bothered to read the instructions properly. I think I know how it works from films and books. Afterwards I read them carefully though. I think I've done it right but I have to read several times what the results mean.

One line means that I'm not pregnant.

The shop floor is grey with black and white dots, randomly, as if someone has spilled paint. I sit in the stockroom at the computer which shows price changes and I start looking at them but then I just look at the floor. Try to see a pattern in the randomness, to see if there is a pair of the square tiles that make up the floor. It becomes hypnotic after a while, because when Stina comes into the storeroom, half an hour has gone: Were there many price changes?

It's something else now, that monotonous work which I previously was lulled by, the simplicity of it which became a comfort. Now I end up thinking, sometimes about something like the floor and sometimes about something different. Something completely different.

Something outside this place.

Sleep like a second skin, enveloping, safe and close. The book slips out of my hand and I don't do anything to stop it. Hear the muffled thud when it lands on the rug. Look at the radio alarm's red numbers. Let my eyes close completely.

73

The grass has turned light brown, almost yellow, the sun hasn't stopped shining this summer. The second summer and I think that I'm waiting for something. For the first time it feels like that.

He has stopped calling when he comes home and I think that it's fine. I think that maybe he doesn't call it home anymore, this place. Maybe it's become only his parents' home now.

Maybe he still thinks that he should call me when he comes here, maybe he wards away the thought but has a slight feeling of guilt.

Although so slight that it is quickly washed out.

One summer evening, it's a little cooler when I leave the shop, but I want to go out for a walk. I dig out a light jacket which I find right at the back of my wardrobe. I don't remember ever having used it since I moved.

It takes a few hours before I make it out, but it's of course still just as light. Even though I think I can see the difference between daylight and the midnight sun now. I go for one of my usual rounds, it usually takes about an hour. On the way home, the air has cooled even more and I stick my hands in my pockets. There's a cinema ticket in the right pocket. At first I think it might be from last year, when I was alone at the coast and went to the cinema, but it's several years old, the text which reveals which film I saw has faded, but when I manage to see what it says I remember all the details. Almost down to which sweets I ate. Another life.

74

As soon as the ice disappears and summer takes over, most people immediately forget the ice. Boats are taken out on the water, bathing shorts are put on. For me, the ice feels close even though the winter is far away. It's not just the snow on the background mountain tops that serves as a reminder, but also the water temperature. It can't get that warm in a lake where there is a thick layer of ice so many months of the year. Not in a lake which is so deep. I never take a bathing costume with me the few times I go down there with Stina. But one time I do swim and it's with Tim the time I let him give me a lift home after the Hotel. I don't know how we get into it, but we start talking about bathing and it's almost one o'clock at night but it could just as easily be one in the afternoon and he drives me to his favourite bathing spot and we haven't said that we're going bathing but when he gets out of the car he takes off everything apart from his boxers and I manage to forget the background, the snow-capped mountains, and I don't think about the ice or the depth and suddenly I've gone in and it can of course be the alcohol but it doesn't feel so cold. Although the next day, when Stina rings to ask if I want to go bathing with her, I don't take my bikini because it feels unthinkable.

The alarm clock's red figures glow towards me when I finally turn out the light. It's later than I would have guessed, I've been reading for more than an hour. I put the book down on the nightstand but in the dark I overreach slightly and the book tumbles down under the bed. I try in vain to reach it.

I'm off the next day and decide to clean. I tidy up the worst of it and then borrow Mona's hoover. Large balls of dust find their way into the vacuum's hose. When I get to the bed I remember the book and crouch down. I can't see it directly, but search for it with my hand under the bed. My hand stops at something soft, paper. I pull out a roll of toilet paper and wonder how it ended up there. Stick my hand under the bed again and find the book. It's dusty and when I vacuum under the bed it rustles, I hear the grime disappearing.

As I'm putting the vacuum cleaner back, it hits me that I used to have nosebleeds every day.

Stina and Lars are a couple now. Not just a couple of people who hang out every weekend and sometimes on other occasions. But a couple who get ready to go out together and eat breakfast together the day after and don't even always come out. But usually they do, of course. The Hotel is everyone's living room on Saturdays. Slightly less grubby since the renovation. But mainly on the outside. Nothing else has changed with the village. Sometimes when Stina and Lars stay

212

home Jenny calls me. I don't have her number, but I save it after the first time. Not to call her, but so that I'll know who's ringing me. She thinks we can go out just the two of us. That we can take my car. These are the times when Kalle is away or has his license suspended. I say yes and pick her up at different pre-parties which are sometimes escalating and sometimes just winding down. Once we get to the Hotel we both disappear off in different directions. Mainly she does. The Hotel on Saturdays is the same as ever. The new décor becomes a part of Saturdays too.

It takes so long for me to come to a decision. One of the biggest arguments is that I'd most probably never come back here again. What would bring me back again?

75

Finn would never buy new alloys for his car. The car is small and red, dark red and often quite dirty. I don't ride in it that many times, he mainly drives between the village and the town where he lives and the school. We finish at the same time this Saturday and there are only a few weeks until he graduates and leaves this place. Maybe he'll never move back, although we don't talk about such distant future. Finn isn't always at the Hotel on Saturdays, mainly because he doesn't live in the village, so he doesn't need to start getting ready for these nights out straight after work. I say yes when he asks if we should go for a drive somewhere.

It's winter-spring and the last of the ice rolls quietly into the lake's edge where we are sitting on a simple wooden bench, each on a plastic bag from the store. Finn smokes one of his hand-rolled cigarettes and I think about how it's him and the Norwegians that do that, roll their own cigarettes. And I think that in Finn's case it's also a way of standing out. Just like the dyed black hair, which often reveals several centimetres of the lighter hair before he gets round to dying it again. We don't say so much, he tells me that he is thinking of just taking a suitcase to London and filling half of it with tobacco because it's cheaper here. I think that he's exaggerating but I don't say anything.

It's only when I'm standing in line at the chemist that I understand that this won't work. The woman at the till who almost only buys vegetables and cakes. And one in the queue who is friends with Kalle. And that I recognise all of them. You don't buy pregnancy tests here.

I wait until the next day, I'm off and it's a week day, I set the alarm to eight, eat breakfast and then get in the car. No one here wonders what I'm doing, no one will ask me where I'm going and why.

In the neighbouring town I park at the large carpark near the bus station and when I'm locking the car, I recognise someone, but only fleetingly and it doesn't matter. Walk along the street where almost all the shops are and find the pharmacy without looking. And don't recognise anyone there. I buy an ice-cream in one of the grocery stores afterwards and then walk back to the car and drive home.

76

The local paper which doesn't have its head office here, but out on the coast, of course writes about the accident. There is a reporter who works here and in the nearby town, who is also the photographer. There is a picture of the scene of the accident and the incident is described clinically and without names. Everyone in the break room reads it thoroughly when they each in turn get access to the paper. An extra copy has been bought in today, one which everyone holds carefully, it will need to look unread and be sold later on. But maybe today we'll touch the newspaper cautiously regardless of what is to happen to it later. There is a tight silence in the room.

Several days later there is a picture of Tim and his mum talks about her grief. There is a whole section, where even a local police officer is interviewed about traffic safety. It is at no point written in black and white and no one says it out loud, but everyone knows that Tim had alcohol in his blood.

I read the articles too, but at home. It's the first time I buy the newspaper here.

Like anywhere else, this place also looks different in the fog.

It's morning and as I'm on the late shift I'm free. For the sake of a change, I've got dressed for work much earlier than I need to and so I go for a stroll. The fog lies close, embedded in the village. Every corner becomes rounder and all the lines less sharp. Nature softens too. I turn off between the villas on the outskirts of the village and end up in a forest where lots of people normally walk their dogs. The nature here is so close to everything that I could almost have felt at home here before. The fog erases the last of that I cannot put into words and welcomes me in some way. Two Labradors bounce around and fetch sticks which are thrown for them.

77

He has changed brand of deodorant but his smell is still basically the same. He gives me a hug which is neither too long or too short, one which shows where we have one another. It is a given that he will be at the Hotel tonight, the market is on, everyone is home. I don't see Emelie, but I assume that she is with him.

We talk a bit about the coast and the inlands, phrases which mean something but not much. Then someone grabs him by the arm, he turns and his smile widens: See you later.

And then he's gone.

The ice underneath me. Suddenly it doesn't feel fragile at all, more like substantial, solid. It's silent and the snow on top helps with the quiet. The silence of nature doesn't feel nearly as aggressive or insistent. At least not today.

78

Just before the snow melts for good is when the pines look at their saddest. The branches are heavy with the wet snow. The snow melts just once here; winter is decisive and never hesitates. And in summer the pines are proud and stand tall, as if they had never been weighed down, but had always stood straight, pointing skywards.

I think a fair bit about Tim after we meet, but not more than that I've almost managed to forget him until that day he drives off the road. You don't forget someone after that. You don't forget someone whose car was sliced in half.

The slope up to the Hotel is deserted. It's Sunday afternoon and no one is on their way here. At the top I park alongside a solitary car in the large carpark. When I'm walking towards the viewpoint realise that I've left the key in the ignition. For the first time.

The view is just as striking as usual. Just as astonishingly powerful after all the days here. All the nights.

The lakes, the forests, the village, the fell. Insignificance, enormity.

On the way back towards the car I see a skip around a corner. An ordinary, blue skip with various objects sticking out. Some of the old faux leather armchairs, a broken table. It's several months since they redecorated the Hotel, but here are the leftovers. I walk closer.

It's the first time I see the bear in daylight. I'd not understood how it really looks. Shoddy, worn out, its gaze far more tired than I could see in the dark of the Hotel's basement. It looks despondently at me.

79

I get a library card. When I have to say my address I'm almost surprised that I know it, it seems strange to hear it. I've not said it out loud very many times. Nor written it down either. But this is still where I live and have lived for more than a year. But I know that I don't belong to that address, know that I'll quickly learn the next one, maybe even forget this one.

I borrow two books, one with a good-looking cover and one by an author whom I've read before. Both are new in and stand on a shelf near the entrance and the issue desk.

It has been a long time since I read a book. I think about my white bookshelf and the books there. The ones that definitely left visible marks in the dust. Untouched since they were put there. Books that I chose to take with me to my new address, to my new life. To my continued life. The one that was maybe put on hold. Or which continued. I decide to actually read these books.

When I drive out into the nature I recognise it. This is how he showed me. First by car and then on foot.

But in spite of my feet landing in the right place this time, it still doesn't work. What worked before, I can't put my finger on. Don't remember that I felt near or included. My feet sink down through the crust when I stand in the same place for too long. If I hurry, then it's ok. Other tracks in the snow everywhere. Mainly from scooters.

I don't know what I am looking for but I feel satisfied with having gone out. In a way it feels good, even if I don't belong here.

The enormous untouched pines with the snow-weighted crowns. The lightness in the air, the silence.

Sonia decides that we should get to have fruit for free at work, to eat on our breaks. When it's time for my coffee break, I go round the fruit and vegetable corner and take some cherries and an apple. I'm on my way towards the break room but turn around when I get to the storeroom. Go to the backdoor and the loading bay. None of the others on the early coffee break smoke, so I'll be alone. I sit on the edge of the loading bay. Let my legs hang down. Feel the concrete against the back of my bare calves. The sun reaches my feet, but the rest of my body is in the shade. The air isn't cold, but the metal edge of the dock feels cool through my dress. I breathe on the apple and rub it against the cloth of my dress. Take a bite and notice the smell of ciga-rettes. Look towards the carpark and see a Norwegian registered car with the door open. A cigarette thrown out and a foot which stubs it out before the door shuts and the car drives off. But the smell lingers even after the apple is finished. I look the other way, towards the street. Recognise the black hair from behind. He is not alone on the bench. The cigarette, hand rolled, in one hand and, I guess, Joachim's hand in the other.

80

The graveyard is separated from the church, next to the church there is no room for anything, there is the stream, the village square, the bridge, the museum, the long distance coaches. The graveyard is instead on the other side of the stream and I've never visited it. I consider doing so this time out, but cannot come up with any good reasons to do so. I can just as well walk past it on my evening stroll.

I make a stew and after having eaten it with a cookery program as background noise I put on a jacket and go out.

It's bigger than I would have thought, bigger than I'd guessed from the road, bigger than I would have thought necessary for this little place. And of course I don't know where Tim is buried and I don't know either why I want to visit the spot, but when I see from a distance a grave with drifts of flowers and masses of candles, I know of course that that is the one.

There is no chance of getting back to sleep. I happened to turn over and see the alarm clock's sharp red numbers and there is barely an hour until I have to get up. That's not enough time to get back to sleep. At least not now that I know what time it is.

I get out of bed and roll up one of the blinds. The light from the street lamp comes in and wakes me more and more, I don't bother turning on any lights.

It's not early for other people, there are people up and about in the village, but I take the car to a place outside. Park next to another car in a clearing by the road, where a path runs into the forest.

I walk in the dark amongst the trees, I know the paths here pretty well. I hear a dog barking a bit further ahead and a quiet breeze moves in between the pines. It's an ordinary Tuesday and nothing special is happening, but there is still something. Me. Here. In the forest. It feels almost like something someone from around here would do.

81

Just like when I walked out on the ice alone for the first time, I go carefully to begin with. It doesn't quite work like getting used to it on foot and actually it's probably safer to drive quickly. I think about when the ice will break up in a few weeks and people will dare each other to drive over the open water on snow scooters. You need to not hesitate, to go for it, to not let go of the throttle. The scooters can handle wide open water. But now it's ice and my faded green car.

I know where the ice road goes, where it's ploughed and churned up and I follow the tyre tracks. Slow at first, but after a while I dare to change up through the gears and step down harder on the gas.

And I know how you skid. Not just in theory, because when I pull on the handbrake I actually skid.

Then I stop and walk out onto the ice. Look towards the village, towards the Hotel and the ski slope and know that this is my last chance to see all this from here, on the middle of the lake.

One Tuesday evening Mona is gone longer than usual and for some reason my thoughts wander. Maybe she dropped her stick, lost her balance, won't be able to carry on living in the house. And by now, I've got to a point where I know that if it were to happen, I wouldn't look for a new place to live. That would be my reason.

A few hours later I hear her hesitant steps, hear her lean the stick against the stairs to go into the kitchen.

82

Tim's car is blue, metallic, and on the track behind the hotel carpark I can see that he has skidded about in it. The car is still neatly parked. The alloys are silver and look expensive. Fredrik has shown me in a catalogue what four alloys can cost, amounts completely outwith my comprehension. The car's interior is also well looked after.

I'm not longing to leave; I just don't want to be here anymore.

83

I'll never answer with an intake of breath.

84

I see the accident site once. It's on a stretch of the road towards Norway, a road I've never driven myself. But one Sunday off, I decide that I want to go there. I know roughly where it is, because I've heard people talk about it. It's been several weeks now and the worst of the vacuum after the accident has given way. People talk more about other things and more about it.

There are candles by the roadside, some of them are actually burning. And flowers, most of them dried or shrivelled. A porcelain angel and some small plush toys which have become grubby. And a picture of Tim, the same photo as in the paper, a several years' old photo from high school. His hair shorter, an even and half smiling expression.

The bark of the tree which halved the car has peeled off on one side. There's a tallish pine which had enough strength to stay standing. I didn't think so much before I came out here. Mainly that I hoped no one would come at the same time as me. But I've brought a bouquet of flowers I bought at Olle's the day before. Olof raised one eyebrow slightly at me buying something other than my usual. I lay the flowers next to the others. Then I get back in the car again and do a u-turn.

On page 171 is a lyric from Enjoy Yourself (It's Later Than You Think) by The Specials, a cover of the original by Guy Lombardo.